Anthology:

David Wakes Up

Vox

The Evolution

Oliver B. Williams

Jacket Design by Oliver B. Williams

ISBN-13: 978-0-578-48776-2

Fiction

Published in the United States of America

10 9 8 7 6 5 4 3 2

ACKNOWLEDGEMENTS

Thanks to Irmgard Williams for her painstaking, meticulous copy editing. Thanks to Avery Williams for her keen, aesthetic perspective as I designed the cover.

DEDICATION

These three works span portions of my life containing many increments of change and development. I'm very pleased with my life, and that of which it is composed. That being said, I'm compelled to dedicate this collection of works to the fissures and detours of my past, locking in the wheels of my course, leading me to this present.

I must dedicate this collection to all my life's errors. An error is only an error if it caused an outcome untoward a planned or designated future outcome. I could not have planned a better future. My perceived errors were not errors at all, although at the instant of experiencing any of the trials and tribulations, I believed I was the worst doofus of all.

Here's to my life's errors. Thank you.

David Wakes Up

Rush hour traffic—this early in the morning? It should be morning. It feels like morning. I just woke up; I hear morning rush hour traffic, but the light isn't right; the sounds aren't right; the cars aren't right. I know the difference between morning and night. When cars go home, the tempo is different. They say: You! Out of my way! You're intruding on my time now, not the company's time. They unwind, easing the spring. The day is done, and I am free. Let me go to my friends, my family, my cozy and familiar environment, where I am not bound by shackles of economic responsibility and laborious role playing. Let me go to where I really do care, and away from this place where my attention, regard, and interest are feigned and contrived.

Nose-close carpet pile and rug dust were not uncommon to David. With his face affixed to the floor, he was in a twilight region of awareness where self and surrounding were indistinguishable. His senses were lost in a blur, blending the uncomfortable dreaminess between awakening from a nightmare and the first few seconds of grogginess in a surgical recovery room. The tactile sensations activated first: lips pressed against the coarseness of the drool and vomit soaked rug; the cool dampness in his crotch. Smell kicked in to revive these first primordial brain functions.

The base level of vision—light perception—eluded David. Language, thought, memory, emotions—these amalgams of humanness had been banished. His awareness consisted of the most primitive of bodily sensations. His brain did not apply form to image, making memory undecipherable. His condition was akin to a prenatal state, where only the sounds of the mother's working viscera, and her surrounding ambiance, offered up any means of distinguishing between self and other.

He had regressed to a level that millions of years of evolution had toiled and erred to overcome. By whatever means self-awareness directs consciousness, he had slithered to the threshold. He was not depressed, elated, happy, sad, guilty, shameful, embarrassed, dejected, forlorn, or bad. His self-imposed underworld held him tightly. Had he died, the transition would have been less remarkable than the death of his 89-year-old grandmother, who went peacefully in her sleep, having had the satisfaction, at whatever level, of the completion of a dream-fired neuron or a REM-induced muscular twitch.

David was neither a contortionist, a Yoga master, a Tai Chi practitioner, nor a Buddhist monk. Yet the juxtaposition of his limbs, torso and head suggested an Eastern mystical persuasion. His body formed an asymmetry that seemed too deliberate–a concerted cosmic misalignment telling the onlooker that perhaps this pose was intentional. An observer might suspect a form of meditative bliss. In sleep one tosses and turns and thrashes about, but David did not budge. His stillness persisted as his memories meandered, flickering in and out of his awareness—cloudy rehearsals of past attempts to alter and divert that which was his life.

A dreamy image materialized. As the memory focused, the corners of his mouth upturned, releasing more drool: Several years ago an ad in *The City Weekly*, the local free rag, caught David's attention. He enjoyed perusing the personals, especially reading and gloating about "all the losers who could not find dates." A recurring display ad, intermingled with the rest, caught his attention:

"Uncover your inner self! Discover who you really are!" the ad boldly challenged.

"Relieve yourself of worldly burdens and open up the real YOU. Discover your unfulfilled psychic being. We promise to open new vistas and horizons of joy for you."

"They've got to be on the level," David pondered. "The ad's been in the 'Health and Healing' section for months." He paid $300 to enroll in Maharishi Nazidora's workshop. "Hell, yes! Instead of me going to Tibet, the wise man came to me," David gloated, rejoicing in all the money he would save in travel expenses. He had fantasized a trek to Tibet, in search of ultimate bliss and truth.

He told women he met at bars and parties he had read W. Somerset Maugham's *The Razor's Edge*; he had only seen Bill Murray in the movie. This transgression of the truth did not affect him–the end justified the means. He had rented the video and cried when Sophie died. When he compared the book to the movie, he insightfully informed listeners that the movie had not captured the essence of the book. Euphorically, he had waxed into fantasy about spiritual bliss and the benefits of unrewarded selflessness to which the film had alluded. He wished he were Bill Murray; he had intended to read the *Upanishads* some day; he had not discovered his hidden self in Maharishi Nazidora's workshop, but he did score a good drug connect.

Mercifully, David's return to wakefulness unraveled slowly, not inducing severe withdrawal trauma. His reviving olfactory and tactile senses hoisted his other senses to gradual recovery. Rudely, however, his remaining senses did not respect the same gradual return to comfort. A crisis of sensory overload ensued.

The floor hummed monotonously. An occasional screech interrupted the asynchronous drone. The vibration ebbed and waned. An angry burst of sound assaulted his ears, like a large mythological bird squawking, threatening trespassers violating its territory. David's head jerked at this intrusion, interrupting his meditative trance.

He turned his head, allowing new odors to trickle in from the outside—reality-laden, smoky perfumes. The persistent drone and the barrage of smells helped boost him from his mime of lifelessness. Sounds and smells foreign and unworldly a century ago now swirled around him, providing a reminder of what lies behind the door. Slauson Avenue hosted David's revival.

Tens, hundreds, thousands of cars plodded along the street, goading him further into consciousness. He opened his eyes to dim, confusing shadows from diffuse sunlight.

Incongruent sensory stimulation: the light, the smells, the sounds, the feel of the air. His internal clock did not match what he felt.

With opened eyes and dawning awareness, he pivoted his head on his chin. His motion was partly reflexive, partly cognizant. He barely averted from the soup oozing from this mouth. The anesthesia had subsided, reminding him of his many hours locked position. He had learned in Maharishi Nazidora's workshop: movement begets awareness. The urine in his pants did not concern him; his current address was of no consequence, nor the time he had spent reposed; even his own identity could, for the time being, remain transparent.

He balanced his head with his chin on the floor, persevering the pain and ignoring the vomit upon which he had settled. His groggy gaze floated across shadowless carpet pile and innocuous patterns. The onset of dusk desaturated the colors, giving the objects a dull pastel appearance. Various items were strewn along his plane of vision. His focus coasted further out: table legs, the bottom of a sofa behind them, a tattered doll, some scattered magazines, keys, an overturned plastic trash can, shards of glass, shoes, an opened book of matches. The book of matches sparked a memory. He strained to read the cover: *Otto's Meeting Place*, red with a yellow background. Abrupt pain in his head jolted him. He cringed, tilting his head to notice an unfamiliar red blotch of texture and color in the carpet.

Was I at Otto's? His body slumped, succumbing to his discomfort, dwelling upon the many occasions he had philosophized from his barstool, proselytizing his insights to those worthy, attractive, and feminine—but not too smart. Intelligent women questioned him, and he could not waste his time engaging in their issues and flaws. So many memories, orating and gesturing from his soapbox barstool: "The difference between awareness and consciousness is rhetorical," he often espoused. And yet another favorite: "The great advancements and discoveries in science did not come from continued replication and variation in the status quo, but rather from the discovery and examination of the contradictions and differences." He churned out variations of these two themes until he changed nighttime haunts and started all over.

He confided to his audience that he is a student of psychology, and he humbly considered himself as a scientist, thinker and philosopher. Being particularly keen about awareness and consciousness, he believed their subtle difference was the ubiquitous thread of Einstein and other discoverers of the universe's mysteries. He had hoped his intelligence and insight would someday reward him with similar just deserves. His pain reinserted itself.

He diverted his current discomfort to memories of a university course—*Attributes of Awareness*—pain, how it is transmitted, how it is perceived, and how the sufferer copes. The professor was a tall, robust, red-headed man with a clear and strident voice. Rather than sit at a desk, or stand behind a lectern, this man stood in the middle of raised platform, a shallow stage. He had arranged his three graduate student teaching assistants in standing formation, flanked in front of him, their arms folded, stoic and taciturn—one at each corner of the platform, and one centered, all on the floor so as to not be at his level. David had mused: *These guys are either bouncers at a rock concert, secret service, guarding a government dignitary, or pathetic middle class neo-Nazis who apparently missed the head-shaving, tattooing and piercing classes required for their stereotype.* Other students in his class had not been so amused, complaining about the professor's presumptive and idiosyncratic style of teaching. But David quipped while sitting with three other students in a coffee shop, "Where else can you get so much entertainment—plus university credit—for the price of a registration fee?" David had exercised exemplary awareness, earning an "A" in the class.

His head throbbed with an indistinct ache, becoming more intense as he lay on the floor. His recollections, connected but loose, meandered to what a therapist in an anxiety management workshop once suggested: pain without an apparent cause is like a persistent, irritating noise in your house in the middle of the night with an unknown source. A feeling of panic gave way to memories of skiing on a cold morning. He had slipped while traversing a steep, icy slope. Unable to edge his skis to stop, he continued to accelerate. He edged and edged, trying to keep from tumbling, trying to slow his decent. His bindings released, and his skis ricocheted away, leaving him without means to control his fall. *I can hit something at anytime; my leg could snap; my head could hit a rock. The same thing that happened to Laura Meeks could happen to me.*

His heart raced as a slideshow of bad images unfolded. Laura Meeks was a friend of his ex-wife's. While skiing at Mammoth Mountain, Laura and her husband had traversed a steep icy slope. She had paused to view the scenery and catch her breath, and edged into the icy incline. In an unforeseen instant her skis slipped from under her, and she sped down the slope. As she picked up speed, she edged and dug her ski into the ice, but to no avail. The wind-resistant, Teflon-smooth fabric of her ski attire greased her acceleration. Her leg hit a rock, snapping her femur in two. As the slide accelerated, her broken leg impacted another rock, severing the leg completely. Onlookers watched as her independent, flailing limb, ski still attached, gyrated uncontrollably to the bottom of the slope, and stopped, ski flat to the surface.

Agony blossomed from within his head. Dull and sharp, constant and intermittent, the variation tortured him. It assailed him with well-executed tactical strategy. He felt it in his temples, behind his eyes, in his forehead, in the neck muscles directly under his skull, under his eyelids, directly between his eyes, and over his nose. A creeping aching and tingling pervaded his limbs. A razor-sharp stinging pierced his toes and feet. As he moved to bear weight on his elbows, prickly spikes invaded his fingers. He had been in the same position for a very long time. Movement hurt; thought of movement hurt.

A different pain assaulted him. It didn't hurt; it came from nowhere. It seeped in insidiously, stealthfully. It was a spy, a gremlin, a misty, bodiless demon, surreptitiously corroding the works. Memories, thought, apprehension, fear, panic, guilt, shame—they gained access, virulently increasing their number. The usurpers came from nowhere, their source and purpose unknown. An onslaught of memories begat segments of thought, spewing out chunks of disconnected fear, panic and distress. David cringed. The usurpers revealed themselves—strident, piercing images from the past. They circumvented words, taking a direct path—a short cut of potency—to the most sensitive and vulnerable area of David's brain, unmoderated by reason and rationale. He tried to hide and cower, to strike out and attack. The bombardment of images found him, intruding memories upon him. *I remember Joe. I was twelve. His mother…she was funny. She could sum things up, especially if me or Joe fucked up. She'd say: Boy! You don't know whether to shit or go blind!* David cracked a smile. *I should have thought of Joe's mother when I was in therapy last week, when he asked me to think of something pleasant in my childhood.*

David had been in and out of therapy most of his adult life–groups, individual sessions, family sessions, couples sessions—he had been there. Pressure drove him to therapy, especially when it came from outside. Bosses, wives, girlfriends, and courts nudged him toward the "cultural messiahs of self-discovery," a phrase he had coined for psychotherapists. One of his least favorite therapists gave him homework. David was irate.

"Homework?! From a fucking shrink! Teachers give homework, not fucking, goddam asshole counselors I'm paying $100 an hour to," David had dissented during a quiet moment over a double martini at Otto's.

His therapist had asked him, "When you suddenly feel blue, what are your thoughts immediately prior to the feeling?"

Well...dipshit...I was thinking that I feel like shit. I need a drink, or a pill, or something other than being here with you.

"Well, doc, I was thinking I don't like my job, and I'm not doing what I want to do in life. And I don't like where I live. And my girlfriend doesn't understand me. That's enough to make anyone take a drink, isn't it?" David responded with formula-like mendacity.

So, the therapist gave him homework. He had to keep a journal, and every time he "experienced a blue feeling," he had to record what he was thinking just prior to the bad feeling. *How can I do this? It's a sea of blue. I can't tell when sadness ends and where it begins, so how do I discern the antecedent?* He had to make stuff up, or else the therapist would say that he was not cooperating, and the probation officer would not be happy.

His journal entries were forthright and uncontrived, chronicling his experiences accurately: "Once I was walking down a street and paused at a crosswalk. A man about my age, driving a new Mercedes convertible, turned the corner in front of me. Without thinking, I suddenly felt bad. No envy or jealousy or hatred for this passing stranger—I simply knew this man was happier than I and, most certainly, had a better life." The image was momentary—a stroboscopic flash too fleeting to identify. It carried a disturbing message to which he answered by slipping into the corner strip mall bar.

Still face down on the floor, David's heart beat faster. A vacuum clamped his stomach. The demon from within attacked him. He would soon be convicted, as he had avoided his execution for too long. Doomed and condemned, they were coming for him. He was defenseless; his vulnerability motivated him to move, lest they come in and carry him away. They had experience dealing with people like him. They knew how he thinks and what he is: a failure, a loser, irresponsible, wretched and undeserving of anything good. He would receive no mercy. He had to move, or else they would gobble him up as they lay there, face down and defenseless.

But should he defend himself—confronting these accusers, these blamers, these indicters—then the next level of hell awaited him. He would take his place among Brutus, Judas and Adolf Hitler (whom he was sure Dante would have also included as a tenant of the depths of Hell).

I must flee; I must seek refuge; I must move. It hurts. Oh my god…it hurts. I've got to get up…off the floor. I'm at home…how'd I get here?

David pushed up, arching his back and torso from the floor from his elbows. He unfurled his legs and pulled his knees forward so that he was on all fours. His head hung between his shoulders like a tired farm animal. Glass chards dangling from his hair dislodged and dropped to the floor, confetti-style. *What's that? Some chick put glitter in my hair last night?* He arched his head upward, then dropped it, succumbing to the pain.

Time? He lifted his head again to get a glimpse at the wall clock: *6:15.* David routinely awoke early in the morning, hung over and jittery from a night's bar hopping. His routine was his last anchor. He took pride in his fortitude and self-control: he got up in the morning, took a shower, dressed in fresh clothing and went to his engineering job—his sixth since he graduated from college. He passed on drinking coffee; it made him feel worse, escalating the shaking. As hung-over co-workers dwindled in on Monday mornings, he gloated, ridiculing them about their lack of resilience.

His emptiness was insidious, as he yearned for something to fill him. He felt parched and barren, craving anything to relieve the abyss. The craving spawned spurious memories, and he recalled discussions with his favorite organic chemistry professor, a fellow who had worked for Jim Beam as a researcher, developing molecules to make grain alcohol taste like aged bourbon. David followed in his professor's footsteps, becoming a chemical engineer himself. Organic chemistry fascinated David, and he took great enthusiasm explaining what he did for a living. Stereochemistry amazed him, especially after he finally comprehended it in college. During his demonstrations he used his hands as molecular models, lecturing from a bar stool. He held his hands forward, arms outstretched, with the back of his hands facing the beset party, usually a tolerant, kind, patient, or comatose woman.

"See my hands? They are both identical, right? Four fingers and a thumb." David set the stage like a magician setting up a card trick. "Yeah, yeah. One hand has a ring on it. Fuck you…you know what I mean." David was sensitive to jokes when he was serious. He shifted his hands over one another, arms outstretched, thumbs protruding, showing the incongruence of mirror images. Later in the evening he would lose some motor dexterity. He would place his hands two inches from his listener's face, or worse yet, hit his listener in the nose. Once he fell off his bar stool. Still, he ended up sleeping with the woman he was trying to impress. They passed out together at David's apartment, not having sex at all. He could at least claim that they had slept together.

David hoisted his torso to a praying position, elbows to thighs, head in hands. His headache had reached its crescendo, but a different affliction disturbed him. He brushed at his hair, dislodging more glass. He recognized the spot on the floor as blood. His name, memory of his childhood, what he did for a living, and the fortunate circumstance that he was at home were his only knowns. Last night did not exist.

Where did this glass come from? What happened to me? These questions seeped out through a surging turmoil, hurting more to focus and concentrate. He was compelled to remember—how could he act without awareness? But he could not recall his most recent experiences. Panic seeped in.

What day is it? What time is it? Where am I supposed to be? Who was I with? What did I do? How did I get here? Why am I on the floor? Why do I have glass in my hair? This blood...it's mine? The pain is great. Do I need medical attention? What if I did something illegal?...Will they know? Are they looking for me?

His questions collided, exploding into anxiety; the shockwave resonating through his being and emptiness. Anxiety, fear, and panic consumed him.

Panic, depression, anxiety...they run together. I don't know which is which. There's a doom out there. It's uncertain, foreboding...it floats out there...a fate awaiting me. Something is bad. I am bad. I am wrong. I'm going to be taken away. I don't know when; I don't know by whom; I don't know for what. Something I did...or didn't do. Maybe it's when I spoke out of turn at the dinner table, and my mother slapped me, or maybe when I asked Doris to have sex with me, and she laughed, or maybe when I didn't ask Norelle to stay the night, and she really wanted to, so I lost out, or maybe it's that money I lost, or the taxes I cheated on, or the people I've lied to, or the jobs I've lost, or the courses I failed, or the life I failed?

A voice spoke to David from the hole within: *Between questions, verbalizations, and your ruminations, images flourish. Imagery eludes verbal capture; the essence of the meaning becomes warped and deluded, masked in symbolism or nonsense. Image is the common denominator—the elemental substance—of thought and memory. It is the stuff infants think; what our ancient ancestors thought. Language is a crude approximation. Remain at the base level. Stay here with me.*

A Gatling gun of words and images besieged him. He cowered, yearning for it to stop. He started to sweat and shiver.

Another memory materialized—he believed a recent one: He had stumbled out to the parking lot in front of the strip mall bar at 2 a.m. He mumbled and cursed under his breath. His gait was not unlike one who had been drinking double vodka screwdrivers and vodka martinis on-the-rocks-with-a-twist since early evening. David was a marathon drinker—a professional. He had practiced and conditioned himself. He knew how to increase his endurance, taking the steroid for the drinking athlete: Speed, Amphetamines, Whites.

"All the money I dropped in this fucking joint…an' they won't gimme one more drink. Fucking assholes. If it wasn't for me, they'd go out of business. Fuck'n dive...fuck'n losers," he mumbled cursing, staggering across the parking lot.

He hunched forward, throwing up on the pavement. David never fared well with vomiting. He heaved and bellowed and spasmed. His performance was worthy of a 911 call, echoing against the night-abandoned stores and shops.

David had not slept for two days. The speed allowed him drink longer; it helped him get through the day as well. He had to get to work and stay there long enough to seem like he was working. The five little pills granting him self-esteem and grandiosity two days ago had lost potency. He could hardly get to his car door. He had taken five more in the bar toilet an hour ago, but the amphetamines had overstayed their welcome.

David's slight, five-foot-nine-inch frame created a scarecrow-looking specter amidst the few cars still parked in the twenty-odd store corner strip mall. Half the store fronts had For Lease signs with out-of-area phone numbers to call for inquiries. The few remaining businesses included a pizza joint, laundromat, hair salon, a video store (significant to David since it was not Blockbuster, and carried porn), a liquor store, real estate office, a place called "Prole's Boutique" (nothing French, Italian, or silk, but lots of brand-bearing baseball caps with plastic bands and shirts with the likes of "Shit Happens" and "The Golden Rule: He Who Has the Gold Makes the Rules"), a chiropractor's office and David's bar. David harbored the notion that he was above drinking there, but he referred to everyone as "my closest friend."

He had craftily parked on the far end of the parking lot, his strategy for avoiding law enforcement entanglement. On occasion the local police had been known for stake outs, nabbing unsuspecting, departing bar patrons as they started their cars homeward bound. This subterfuge outraged David, especially after having been apprehended in this manner himself a few months earlier. With his car parked some distance away, he could survey the area as he walked. Should law enforcement spot him while en route to his vehicle, he would feign walking home and bypass his car.

What David lacked in courage, he compensated with tenacity. And this night he was determined to point himself homeward. He struggled from his sickly respite, attempting to gain further ground. He had passed out in his car too many times—in too many parking lots and strange neighborhoods. He had awakened to the ridicule of curious school children knocking on his car window, laughing, or yelling, "Mommy! There's a dead man in the car!" No more would he accept the admonishing glances of early shoppers peering at him, having been unaware of the occupant in the parked car their door had bumped. He was going home. He was going to awake in familiar surroundings.

Upon arriving at his car, he yanked at the door handle, cursing himself for locking it. "If someone is stupid enough, or hard up enough to steal this piece of shit, they can have it," he justified for purposefully not locking his car door most of the time. " If they want it bad enough, they'll just bust the windows and take it anyway. Then, if they don't steal it, I gotta deal with busted windows and cold ass wind at night. So, why lock it?"

Groping in his pocket, he withdrew his keys, grumbling that they were misplaced, as he was very particular about what went in which pocket. Keys on key ring always in right pants pocket; coins in left pants pocket; wallet always in left rear pocket; cell phone in right rear pocket. Pants without pockets, or too few pockets, were pragmatically unfashionable to David. A twice-fucked girlfriend, (David's intimacy gauge), a flight attendant, suggested that he carry a bag, so he could wear more stylish pants. Politically correct David silently referred to such accoutrements as "fag bags." He scoffed at the idea, replying that his employers would frown upon such an accessory. He never called her again. Flight attendants were stigmatized from then on.

Tiny, jagged, engravings circumscribed the car door keyhole. He jabbed with his car key— three, four, five pokes, and success. He cursed at the door lights. He especially hated the kind that stayed on after you closed the door. He knew someone, somewhere, was lurking, looking, checking him out, wondering. Dark was better—he was safe. He started the engine.

He felt relieved, having recalled part of the evening. Drenched in sweat, he sat cross-legged on the floor. He still had no idea how he got there, nor did he care. The unfamiliar glass chards, though uncomfortable, were a distant concern. Bright lights and clashing sounds screeched momentarily into his consciousness and disappeared. Wobbly and unsteady, he stood.

I can't continue to live like this. I wake up on the floor with piss in my pants. I hurt so bad I can't think. I don't know if it's morning or night.

Pulling his watch from his pocket, he confirmed it was evening. *I slept all day. I missed work. What will I tell them? I was sick?...No...I had an accident?...OK. How did I get home? I don't remember driving home...I don't remember coming home...I don't remember how I got here...Where are my keys?*

He lumbered across the room, squeezed by the coffee table and fell backward into the sofa. He slumped forward and grimaced. Elbows on knees, he held his face in his hands.

How terrible. I can't remember. I remember the floor...I remember the parking lot. I threw up. What happened next? It's a blank. Oh...I'm sick...It's bad...I can't...I can't. My car...!

David's parking stall was directly behind his apartment, visible through his bathroom window. Panicked about his car, he sprang up, banging his shin on the coffee table.

"Fuck!" he screamed, hobbling to the bathroom. He fumbled with the stuck window latch, pinching his thumb while forcing it open. He slid the window to its security stops, exposing a four-inch gap. He kneeled down and extruded his head through the narrow window slit, attempting to get a glimpse of his car. It was there, parked head in, so he could only see the back half. He pressed his face harder, so the skin bunched up around his ears. He could see the front end was damaged, the extent to which he could not ascertain. His heart raced. He wanted it to go away.

The emptiness overwhelmed him. He did not want to die—he wanted his life to be different. Suicide was not an option; he did not want to die. Cowardice? Narcissism? Fear of the unknown? He did not know. He preferred living. Dichotomy was the source of anguish: he loved life; he hated life. He savored the taste of Chicken Scaloppini, swooned in the aroma of night blooming jasmine, delighted in the sensation of ocean spray massaging his face while sailing, smiled at the cool caress of a late afternoon fog rolling onshore. He marveled at the laughter and glee of children playing.

How many times have I stood here? I have a choice. How many times can I choose? How many times can I make the same decision? I haven't kept count. Once or an infinity, it makes no difference. Is my life so eroded I cannot leap the rut?

He clasped the bottle, unaware of the brand and pedigree. He spun off the cap unceremoniously with a single motion. His body reacted accordingly: jaw muscles tightened; throat and stomach braced for the offensive. He tipped his head back to apply the salve. His face distorted to the unseemly medicine. It burned, not of heat, nor of spicy jalapeno, but an antiseptic burn on a wound. It etched a path gliding through. It diffused, spreading its ghostly presence. He waited for salvation.

Vox

Here is an ageless tale, though seldom told in the open—the wise, mindful of mocking the formidable power invoked by a child's wish. This chronicler must take exception, risking relating this tale, as it must be told to balance the observed with the unobserved, the measured with the immeasurable. Similar events have happened not *upon a time*, as many such stories begin, but *upon many times and in countless places*. At one time and place, a wonderful, smart and beautiful girl named Avery lived in a gray and white house near the beach with her mom, dad and brother. Her room—a very special room on the second floor—was warm and cozy, filled with lots of engaging and interesting items, all chosen and placed by her own hands. Maps and posters of all the places she had visited—or wanted to visit—lined her walls. Her stuffed animals shared the bookcase with her books; her computer sat atop her desk; her drawing board dominated the center of her room. Avery played games on her computer; she watched movies; she read her books; she solved her jig-saw puzzles; she studied her maps; she wrote on her drawing board. She enjoyed doing so many things, and she had no complaints. Well—just one—she did not have enough time in the day to do all the things she wanted to do. She woke up in the morning, and before she knew it, her mom and dad were reminding her it was her bedtime.

Avery thought—as was often her nature to do: *If only I did not have to go to sleep so early, I would be happy. I would have enough time to do everything I love to do: I could finish my puzzles, watch my movies, write on my drawing board, and play more games. I need more time.*

Going to bed and sleeping were, indeed, Avery's biggest problems. "Avery!" her mother would say, "Stop what you're doing, and get ready for bed. It's bedtime!…Now!"

Avery didn't even look at the clock; she knew what time it was when she heard those words. And she didn't like those words at all.

"Mom, can I stay up just ten minutes longer? Pleeeeeeze?" She could elongate "please" without taking a breath for at least fifteen seconds.

"No, Avery. You know tomorrow is a school day. You need your rest. Please, do as I asked, and get ready for bed. And be sure you brush your teeth one minute longer for the extra candy I know your dad slipped you!" her mother curtly reminded her.

Avery snuck downstairs to plead with her dad. "Can I stay up fifteen minutes longer? Pleeeeeeze?"

He looked up from his book and studied her face. At first she thought he might relent, since he was very much like her, and had already given in to her request for extra candy, but firmly said, , "No, Avery. Tomorrow is a school day. You need your rest. Besides, didn't I just hear your mother tell you to get ready for bed? And be sure to brush your teeth a little longer because of the candy I gave you," Avery's dad added.

Avery slumped back up the stairs, disappointed about having to go to bed. She had so much more she wanted to do today. *If only I had more time*, she thought to herself.

So, she dutifully, but begrudgingly, got herself ready for bed: she put her clothes in the dirty clothes basket; she washed her face and hands; she brushed her teeth; she put on her pajamas; she brushed her hair.

"Ready!" she yelled out, knowing her mom and dad would come up to tuck her in…and check: her window was closed, her computer was off, her lights were out, and her überkopf blanket was securely over her head. And each parent came upstairs, doing exactly as they had done every night…for many, many nights.

But this night was different; Avery had an idea. Maybe she could stay awake without anyone knowing, just to see what would happen. Still, she wouldn't be able do all the things she liked to do— her mother or her father or her brother would hear her moving about in her room. They'd tell her to get back into her bed and go to sleep.

"If only I could stay awake longer, do all the things I want to do, and go to bed later," Avery pondered silently, as she squirmed around in her bed, trying to find a comfortable position. "Problem is, my family would hear me." Avery, being a tenacious girl, continued pondering her dilemma: "Tonight I'm staying awake! What is sleep?" she questioned herself. "It's nothing other than closing your eyes at night while you're in your bed. So, if I don't close my eyes, I won't go to sleep." She had it all figured out.

She pretended to go to bed, but she stayed awake; she refused to close her eyes. In fact, she even stuffed tissues tightly into her eyes so her eyelids would not shut. She couldn't see, but at least she wouldn't sleep. Time ticked on. She remained silent as a mouse and listened outside her room to make sure her mom and dad and brother did not hear her awake.

At midnight her dad came up to check on her and give her a final goodnight kiss. She heard him coming and quickly removed the tissues from her eyes, stuffing them under her pillow. Then she pretended to be asleep. He kissed her on her cheek, tucked her in again, and then went downstairs to go to bed himself.

Avery stayed up longer and longer. When she felt herself drifting off to sleep, she pinched her arm. "Ouch!" she whispered loudly, but she wanted to yell.

From outside her bedroom window she heard fewer cars, fewer airplanes flying overhead, absolutely no voices, and the sounds of the ocean were clear and unfettered. "It must be very late," she thought. Suddenly, she startled, hearing scratching noises from inside her closet. She sat straight up in her bed. The last time she had heard similar noises—little animals moving around, or tiny fingernails clawing at her closet door—her brother was playing tricks on her, trying to scare her. "It can't be Adrian because he's fast asleep," she concluded aloud.

"What is that noise?" she wondered. Being a curious child, she felt around on her nightstand, grabbed her flashlight, turned it on, ventured out of her bed and peeked into the closet, shining the light into the darkness.

"Who's there?" she whispered, careful not to make much noise.

The scratching continued, becoming more bothersome, as if the perpetrator wore wooden clothing, and was making a path through thorns or leafless vegetation.

"Be quiet in there," she ordered. "If you make too much noise, my mom and dad will wake up."

The scratching stopped, and a faint voice from the closet beckoned her. "Are you Avery?" the voice questioned. "I'm here to help you with your problem," the screechy little voice explained.

Avery was shocked at first. How could a voice—especially a voice with no substance—be in her closet? She shined the light all around—nothing. She wanted to run away, to get her mom and dad, but she stood her ground.

No silly voice in my closet is going to scare me out of my room, she assured herself, ignoring her shaky knees. *I'm staying here to find out what this is all about!*

"Who are you? What are you doing in my room?" she whispered in a demanding tone. "And— what are you doing in my closet this late at night? How'd you get in there, anyway?"

"Are you hard of hearing, little girl?!" the voice responded. "I already told you. I'm here to help you with your problem," the voice answered rudely.

Avery was dumbfounded. She either had to run away to get help, or stay there and deal with a silly, scratchy voice with no body and no name.

"My problem?" Avery exclaimed defiantly, but still aware of her volume. "My problem is there's a weird voice in my closet late at night. Who are you? Show yourself this very instant," Avery sighed loudly, still concerned someone would hear her and scare the voice away.

"I'm Vox...and I'm NOT your problem. Your mom and dad making you go to bed before you are ready—that's your problem. At least that's what you think every night before you go to bed. I've been listening. I listen to the brightest and most persistent children. You have complained exactly two thousand, three hundred and seventy three times—every night since you were three years old. Am I right, or not?" The voice paused briefly for a response; Avery did not answer. "If I'm incorrect, then I'll be off right now, and you'll never hear from me again," the voice threatened, seeming to know more about her than she knew about herself. "I have visited many children for many millennia on many worlds. You are not the first, so do not waste my time!"

For the first time in her nine-and-one-half years of life, Avery was without words. She had forgotten about being scared of the voice; now she was more concerned that the voice had been hearing her thoughts—and for so long. "Vox? What a funny name. Why haven't I seen you before? How could you know what I'm thinking?" Avery implored, raising her voice just a little louder than she wanted to.

"Do you want answers, or do you want help?" the voice replied, not willing to give her the answer she requested.

Help? Avery considered the question thoughtfully. *How can a voice in a closet help me? Especially a voice without arms and legs and a head and a body?*

She hesitated, and then she remembered what her dad had reminded her: Stop arguing so much. Say "yes" sometimes—except to strangers!

But then, a voice in a closet is not a stranger. It can't do anything anyway. It can't hurt me—it has no hands or feet.

"OK," Avery said. "What will you help me with? My homework? I already know how to do my homework."

"Be serious, little girl. If I can read your thoughts, certainly I already know you can do your homework. No, I'm going to help you with something you want very much—something you cannot do by yourself. I can give you extra time at night, so you can stay up later, and you can go to bed whenever you like."

She knew her dad was a trickster. He made up stories sometimes, looking to see if she could tell the difference between reality and fantasy. Her dad's face gave him away, always revealing a little grin—no matter how serious he tried to be—if the story wasn't real. "Daddy, I know it's you. Quit playing around!" Avery demanded in an even louder hushed voice.

"I'm NOT your father, little girl. I'm the voice in the closet, here to help you get what you've wished for one thousand, six hundred and forty three times," the voice said harshly. "And I must say, you certainly do not seem very appreciative."

Avery shook and jiggled her flashlight, as it was getting dimmer and dimmer. She and her dad had just changed the batteries. Once again she cast the beam all around her closet and in all the corners of the room. Nothing. "Yes, I want your help. I

47

don't want to go to bed so early. I want to go to bed when I want to go to bed," Avery whispered, hissing almost like a snake.

"Very well. Here's the deal. Are you ready to listen?" the voice asked, sounding a bit like her fourth grade teacher before she started a lesson in her classroom. As she readied herself to listen to the voice's instructions, she snapped her mouth shut, suddenly remembering her parents' frequent reprimand about not watching TV with her mouth open. She turned off the now dim flashlight; the batteries were so weak, the light was barely yellow. The room was dark except for the faint light from the streetlamp peeking through her blinds.

"Whenever your parents say it's your bedtime, all you have to say is: 'I wish I had more time.' When I hear those words, I'll give you thirty more minutes." The voice paused, allowing Avery to comprehend the instructions.

She loved what the voice had just told her— but something seemed wrong. She recalled what her dad had told her many times: *When something seems too good to be true, then something is wrong. Always question; always doubt. You don't get something for nothing.*

"What do I have to do in return for this favor?" Avery asked cautiously, not wanting to insult the voice, or make it think she was not grateful for the offer. "My dad told me I can't get something for nothing."

"Your dad is correct, and you are a wise child for remembering what he told you. I will not deceive you; payment is required; you have to pay me back. If I give you time from sleep, then you must to repay my services—with sleep," the voice explained with a matter-of-fact tone.

Avery's jaw dropped again. This time she coaxed it closed with her left hand. She had thought maybe she could pay the voice with some of the money in her piggybank—but with sleep?

The voice detected Avery's doubt and cut her off before she could express her worry. "Tell you what. Did your mother ever take you shopping for shoes?"

"Well, of course," Avery answered indignantly, wondering what kind of stupid voice is this, anyway.

"Well. What happened during these trips to the shoe store? You tried the shoes on before your mother bought them for you. Am I right?" the voice declared, not waiting for Avery to answer. "So then, I'll give you a sample of my services. That way, you can 'try them on' before you make your decision. How's that?"

Avery pondered the voice's offer for a few seconds. It still seemed too good to be true, but she figured her mom and dad would certainly approve, as she was merely being a wise shopper. "That sounds like an OK deal to me," Avery replied, toning down her enthusiasm so as not to let on that she really, really liked the idea. "But, the sample is free—right?"

"Absolutely free," the voice confirmed. "No strings attached."

She thought she had heard an evil, little snicker, but she ignored it. "When do we start?"

Avery asked. She was excited about the free sample, but her dad's warnings still stirred in the back of her mind; however, she remembered trips to the shopping mall as well. While walking through the food court, people in paper hats from behind the counters thrust toothpicks at her, skewered with free samples of food. Her dad didn't complain about those free samples—he chowed down.

"We start tomorrow night. Remember— when your mother or father tells you to get ready for bed, just say: I wish I had more time," the voice said.

Avery waited for the voice to tell her more, but silence followed.

The next morning Avery's alarm clock was as punctual as usual, reminding her that her day awaited. She was groggy at first, hiding her head under her quilt, knowing that her dad would be upstairs soon to prepare coffee and breakfast.

"The voice!" she suddenly recalled. She leapt from her bed—quilt, sheets, pillow, and stuffed animals flying asunder—and ran to her closet—nothing. She opened her blinds, letting the morning sunlight peer in—still nothing. She moved one side of her closet's sliding door open, and cautiously side-stepped inside, pressing her bare foot on a toy she had tossed there (instead of putting it away as her mom had asked her to do). "Ouch!" she yelped.

"Avery!" her dad called her from the kitchen. "I hear you up. Are you OK? Get ready for school. You want waffles or pancakes?"

"Yes, daddy. I'm OK. Waffles, please," she replied, rubbing her aching foot against her ankle. She tip-toed to the other side of her closet, this time taking care where she stepped—no voice, not even a hint of a murmur or whisper. "Was it a dream?" she mumbled.

She exited her closet from the other side, still looking around for any other hints to verify what was probably a dream. Then she spotted her flashlight on her desk. "That's where I put it when I was talking to the voice!" she thought loudly. She picked it up as if it were a rare dinosaur bone she had found in a Sahara Desert archeological dig. She flicked the switch—no light beam; the tiny curlicue of a filament barely glowed yellow.

"It was no dream!" she concluded, clinching her fists and bouncing on her toes. "We just changed those batteries. I didn't use the flashlight except for last night while I was talking to the voice." She became energized, shaking off the sleepiness from when she awoke. She dashed into her bathroom, ripped off her pajamas, scrubbed her face and hands, brushed her teeth (with the electric toothbrush her dad preferred), donned her school clothes, brushed her long, thick, wavy hair (an extra two minutes so her mom and dad would not complain about tangles), put on her clean but not-as-comfortable shoes, tying the laces extra tight, so they would not come loose during the ride to school (causing her to re-tie her laces just as she was getting out of the car at school while everyone in the car line waited behind them), put her dirty clothes in the basket, skipped into the kitchen, hugged and kissed her mom and dad, sat at the table (instead of insisting upon eating in front of the TV while watching Jimmy Neutron or Sponge Bob), finished all the food on her plate (without licking up the excess syrup, a behavior that her mom eyed with disdain), rinsed her dishes in the sink, washed her hands (again), noted the time (seven-fifteen) and announced that she still had twenty minutes to watch television, but she preferred to practice her multiplication tables on her drawing board in her room instead, to which she whisked off and closed the door.

Avery's day was as flawless as flawless could get: the freeway was, for once, free, and dad didn't complain about the traffic; Avery did not have to re-tie her laces before she got out of the car; Mrs. Allen, waiting for her as their car drove up, greeted her with the biggest smile Avery had ever seen. Later that day, Avery listened attentively to everything Mrs. Luna, her fourth grade teacher, taught her; she had three tests—spelling, arithmetic, and reading—all of which she received one hundred percent. And during all her breaks, recesses, and after-school care, she got along fabulously with all her friends—no disagreements whatsoever. What made this day different from any other day? She could not wait for bedtime.

Her mom picked her up from school at the usual time. Avery promptly and politely bid farewell to her classmates, picked up her jacket, backpack, and lunch pail, got into the car, put on her seatbelt without muss or fuss and cheerily announced she was ready to go.

Once home, she did her homework immediately without prompting, coercing, or scolding. She ate all her dinner with no complaints, washed her hands and retired to her room to play computer games. Her mom and dad looked at one another, shrugging their shoulders.

"Interesting phase," her dad commented, seeming neither impressed nor concerned. Her mom, on the other hand, teetered between worry and glee.

The inevitable arrived—those all too familiar words arose from outside her room:

"Avery, get ready. It's bedtime," her dad said after knocking on her door and peeking in.

All day, Avery had convinced herself that the voice was not a dream. Her spirits were high; her expectations just as lofty. Suddenly, she felt as if disappointment loomed close-by. She was in middle of a new game, one on which her brother had tutored her, involving the use of both hands and multiple fingers at the same time. She had almost mastered the skill when her father had interrupted her. "Here goes," she thought. She formulated the words, a mantra she had pronounced so many, many times before: "I wish I had more time."

She said the words half-heartedly, not really knowing what to expect. Usually she said the words in earshot of her parents. She looked from her computer monitor, noticing her dad still poised in her door. He was not moving. She braced for his next word: "Now!" Instead, he just stood there, saying and doing nothing.

"OK, dad, just a couple minutes. I'll close the game," she said, hoping to head off the unavoidable. Her dad remained in her door, still and quiet.

He's got to be messing with me, she thought. "OK, daddy!" she yelled. "Stop it! I'm moving. You can go now!" But her dad was blank, like one of those dressed-up dummies behind the windows in the front of the clothing stores in the mall. She sprang from her chair and ran to her dad to hug him, hoping that might jar him from this nerve-wracking intrusion; he was like a statue.

Avery panicked. She had witnessed her dad behave oddly, but this was, indeed, the oddest she had ever seen. "Daddy! What's the matter?" Her dad was motionless and speechless. "Mommy!" Avery screamed. "Something's wrong with Daddy!"

She flew down the staircase, bounding two to three stairs at a time (behavior that at any other time would be severely frowned upon). Her mom sat reading her students' essays, sporting the disgruntled and irritated expression she bore when engaged in that weary part of her profession: college teacher.

"Mommy. Mommy. Come quick! Something's wrong with Daddy. He's not moving. He's frozen, like a statue!" Avery grabbed her mom's arm, urging her to accompany her upstairs to see for herself. Her mom did not budge, nor did the expression on her face change. She maintained the same statue-like appearance as her dad upstairs. She tugged some more, but her mom did not respond.

Avery was very scared, crying, "Mommy, what's the matter? Why aren't you moving?" But at that very same instant, she noticed her mother's hand-made, heirloom, German wall clock with the precision, pendulum-motion, fine-tuned spring settings and balanced weights—its intricacy recited to her on several occasions in order to stress the importance of "hands off"—had completely stopped. Not just stopped—the pendulum was stuck to one side as if something were holding it from swinging back and forth. She looked at her mother's computer monitor: the usually rapidly moving screen saver was motionless.

Avery bounded back up the stairs to her brother's room, bursting through the door without knocking. Adrian sat in his desk chair, unfettered by her abrupt and unannounced entry. He had contorted his limbs and torso to best facilitate placing his college books and notes on his lap and desk while playing World Of Warcraft on his computer. Avery was always impressed with her brother's physical and mental agility, but this time she was more concerned with her parents' apparent suspended states.

"Adrian. Adrian. Come quick!" she pleaded, grabbing him by his sleeve. Like her father and mother, Adrian remained static. His hands, typically nimble and quick on his mouse and keyboard, were locked in position. The sounds of spell blasts, sword slashes, and melee attacks were blatantly absent, and his monitor displayed a motionless splattering of colors and shapes.

Avery's dismay suddenly vanished. She realized: The voice in the closet wasn't a dream; she recognized the voice had been true to its word—to grant her absolutely free extra time—unhindered time to do as she pleased. She had wished for extra time, and she got it. *What do I want to do? What was I doing before daddy told me to get ready for bed? Well, it doesn't matter. I can do whatever I want now,* she pondered self-confidently, still standing next to her frozen brother.

"Apple cider—in a long-stemmed glass!" she drawled, as if chanting a spell, and she ran to the refrigerator. Sparkling apple cider was her favorite drink, and she was allowed the treat only during special holiday occasions under a watchful parental eye (her dad had demonstrated how a low, flat glass did not tip easily, and the long-stemmed glass was more prone to tipping, a phenomenon he called "center of gravity"). But it made no difference—center, left, or right of gravity—she was going to do as she pleased and enjoy sparkling apple cider from a clear, crystal, long-stemmed glass.

After she had finished sipping her cider—without spilling a drop—she switched on the family television and watched the dreaded Hannah Montana, a program that her parents bemoaned at any and all occasions. She felt so guilty about this transgression, she could not keep from looking over her shoulders, fearful that her family really was not frozen in time; they were only play-acting and would catch her in the act shortly.

She had become comfortable in her freedom, unaware of the passage of time, since all the clocks had stopped anyway. A firm hand touched her shoulder. "Avery! What are you doing? How'd you get in here? And watching Hannah Montana? I told you to get ready for bed," her dad announced firmly, scolding her for not obeying him.

Avery sprang straight up in the air, not knowing she could jump so high without using her feet and legs, startled by her dad's sudden thawing. She felt a mixture of relief and remorse. After all, she had been willing to let her family remain frozen in time while she had her way with the household.

"I...I...I thought maybe you'd let me watch a little more TV before I went to bed," Avery responded with cat-like reflexes. She was as quick to think of excuses as she was quick in her schoolwork. "A trait with mixed blessings," her mom had once remarked

"Get to bed...now!" he demanded, emphasizing the urgency, and pointed down the hall toward her bedroom.

Running toward her bedroom, she remembered immediately that her extra time had limits: thirty minutes. She had wasted much of it just figuring out what had happened, but even so she had a pretty good sense of time; about thirty minutes had elapsed from when she first uttered the words, "I wish I had more time."

She was unsure about hearing from the voice again that night: on one hand, she wanted to verify its existence—to make sure it was not a dream— even though she had firsthand experience of its handy-work; on the other hand, she was still a little frightened. After all, it was a voice in the closet. But, most importantly, she really needed her sleep tonight. She had a crucial arithmetic test in Mrs. Sanchez's class, and if she received another perfect score, that would make ten in row.

Avery's slumber that night was peaceful and undisturbed. The excitement of a frozen family must have tired her out. She did not remember her mom or dad checking on her one last time before they retired for the evening, nor did she recall her brother coming home late from wherever he was and closing his bedroom door. She awoke the next morning spry, alert and ready for the day. She didn't even get drowsy during the ride to school. And for the second time in a row she did not have to re-tie her laces before getting out of the car. She kissed her mom and dad good-bye, backpack in hand and walked swiftly inside her school.

When it came time to take her arithmetic test, Avery was ready. She had practiced adding and subtracting tens and hundreds on her drawing board all week; she knew what she was doing. Avery complied readily when her teacher told the class to put their notebooks and study materials in their desks.

"Hey, little girl. What's yer name again? Oh, yeah. It's Avery. Well, it's payback time," a familiar voice emerged from inside her desk. She looked around self-consciously, startled that the students near her didn't hear it also. "No, they can't hear me," the voice explained, noticing her bewilderment. "And if they could, then it would be payback time for them as well. You really didn't think you were going to get that extra time last night for nothing, did you?" the voice remarked in an even harsher tone than when it was in the closet. Avery's dad had once told her part of his job was working with people who heard voices, but the voices were not real—only to the people who heard them. Avery was beginning to believe she was one of those people.

But the voice had to be real. Look at what it did last night—Dad, Mom, Adrian—all frozen for half an hour, she thought, silently consoling herself, still feeling an urgency about what to say to a voice in her desk while in the middle of her crowded classroom. "Maybe if I ignore it, it will go away, or come back at a more convenient time. It was supposed to be a free sample, anyway," she whispered. Abbie, the girl sitting next to her, looked as if Avery were talking to her, and she shook her head, reminding Avery it was test time.

"Does anyone not have a test sheet?" Mrs. Zimmer asked the class. She paused, waiting for a response. "OK, then, you have one half hour to complete your exam. Please begin," she said.

A loud and unnatural sound erupted from the center of the classroom.

SNORE... SNORE...SNORE... SNORE... SNORE....

Avery's head rested on her desktop, her hands folded neatly as a pillow. She was fast asleep, snoring as she had never done before. The family of birds with a nest in a tree on a branch over Avery's classroom window, departed hurriedly—Avery's snoring was so loud. Dogs and cats for blocks around, barked and meowed in desperation, probably fearing the animal making such an earsplitting sound. The "Quiet Please" signs near the hospital close to Avery's school vibrated and shuttered at the deafening intrusion. The traffic on Las Posas came to a halt. Mrs. Allen, the principal, alarmed by the sound, rushed to the classroom, but she was pushed back by the thunderous commotion inside. Papers, books, pencils, and even Elsie Little and Bobby Slight, the smallest children in the class, were hurled around the room in hurricane-like fashion. Mrs. Zimmer and the other children held their desks tightly, wishing to avoid the same fate. Avery remained steadfast at her desk, undisturbed and serene, except for the snoring.

Mrs. Allen, unable to enter the classroom, and unable to determine the source of discombobulation, called 911. Within five minutes, five fire trucks and five police cars were on the scene. In order to enter the classroom, the firemen engaged special equipment for managing raging firestorms. They escorted each child outside, snatched Elsie Little and Bobby Slight from the maelstrom and coaxed Mrs. Sanchez to release the vice-like clutch she had maintained on her desk. The firemen, now suspecting Avery was the source of the problem, approached her from behind riot shields. They used megaphones and loudspeakers, trying to wake her, but she continued sleeping and snoring in bliss, pausing momentarily to turn her head.

After exactly thirty minutes she awoke, yawning, stretching and smacking her lips, looking around as if she had taken a restful nap on a Sunday afternoon.

"Where is everybody?" she asked drowsily, searching for the rest of her classmates with sleepy eyes. Startled by the disappearance of her classmates and all the activity outside, she jumped out of her seat. The firemen were lined-up tandem from Avery to outside the classroom door. The fireman closest to Avery—apparently ready for a fierce battle—wore a helmet, a protective face guard, fire-proof coat and pants and held a clear shield in front of him—a shield used for mob control. Throngs of well-trained and physically-fit emergency personnel remained on the ready to remove a menace and safety hazard: a nine-year-old girl who happened to snore rather loudly while taking an impromptu nap.

"Do you snore that loudly at home little girl?" the fireman asked her, daring to drop his shield and turn off his megaphone.

She was completely bewildered. Last thing she remembered, it was test time. She just hoped she had gotten another perfect arithmetic score. "Snore?" she answered, insulted by the insinuation. "I don't even snore when I'm asleep, so why would I snore when I'm at school?" she replied, unaware of the events that transpired during the last half hour. "What's going on? Why are we having a fire drill during test time?"

By now Avery's parents had arrived, as Mrs. Allen had called just about everyone except the National Guard, and they were next on her list. Her mom and dad raced by the firemen and other on-lookers, pushing and shoving people aside. They thought something bad had happened to their little girl, but there Avery sat, the center of attention.

"What happened?" her mom asked.

"Avery!" her dad cried. "Are you alright?"

Avery squirmed around in her desk chair, feeling both confused and irritated. "Am I alright? Sure, I'm OK. Why are you guys here? And why is everyone staring at me?" Avery asked, puzzled.

Her mom and dad picked Avery up, hugged her and looked her over carefully. "You aren't sick? What were you doing?" her mom inquired.

"Doing?" Avery responded somewhat defiantly. "I was taking a test."

Avery's dad turned somber and serious, as he quickly became very suspicious of the whole ordeal. A commotion had ensued as the chief of police and the fire chief had pushed through the crowd to join them.

The police chief, Bob, was a tall, pudgy man with red hair, a moustache and a bulbous, hanging belly obscuring the front half of his holster belt. His moustache was slightly uneven, causing Avery's dad to be distracted by the man's upper lip as he talked to him.

"How can a little nine-year-old girl create the commotion you described?" her dad asked. "You're all intelligent people. Does your response really make sense to you? Perhaps you over-reacted. Whatever created the disturbance is gone, but maybe you should investigate the cause before it happens again," Avery's dad suggested to the two city officials. He was pointedly annoyed that adults charged with responsibility could be misled to such a silly conclusion. "Pipes, underground disturbance, sonic boom, earthquake, jets overhead, nearby construction, a passing teenager with a super-charged boom box—almost anything provides a plausible explanation—but not a nine-year-old girl snoring in the middle of the day!"

Chuck, the fire chief, had remained silent while Avery's dad ranted—he was focused on the police chief's unbalanced moustache as well.

Fireman Chuck had removed his helmet as he had approached Avery's mom, the gesture of a man with good upbringing. But, in so doing, he exposed a head almost void of hair, except for the few extremely long strands he had combed over from the side, a feeble attempt to camouflage an otherwise glistening dome.

Chuck and Bob bore sheepish expressions as Avery's dad's reproach was unavoidably indisputable. "Please forgive this unfortunate intrusion," Policeman Bob replied, eyeing the fire chief distrustfully. "What you say, sir, makes perfect sense, and you are correct," he retorted, shooting a scolding, judgmental glance at Fireman Chuck. "If the police department had made the decision, we would have known to look elsewhere."

"If the police department had been here first, they would have arrived with guns drawn," Fireman Chuck responded angrily to Policeman Bob's inferred blame. "AND I don't think that would have been appropriate with a room full of fourth graders!" The two men faced off, staring at one another crossly.

Mrs. Allen had been outside answering questions for the news teams who had arrived on the scene. As she scurried inside to join the group, she overheard the two men quarrelling.

"Gentlemen, you and your teams have both done outstanding jobs here," she interceded with the diplomacy of a boxing referee. "Shortly after your arrival, the commotion stopped, so you must have had something to do with it."

Both Fireman Chuck and Policeman Bob grumbled, muttering indiscernible insults under their breaths. Both wilted from the room, each instructing his respective team to pack up and leave. Later, both meandered toward the news crews, each to detail his account of the incident.

Avery's mom and dad were kneeling by her, consoling her for the scare she had just suffered. Her parents praised her for not being frightened while all these people in uniforms raced about, looking for whatever they were looking for. Mrs.

Allen lingered by them, looking confused herself. "I'm going to call all the parents, and close school early today," she told Avery and her parents. "I don't think we can get much done after all that excitement. The children are too wound up—even in the other classrooms."

Avery silently rejoiced as she and her parents walked across the parking lot to their car and drove home. Because the school day ended early, Mrs. Sanchez did not assign any homework. Nevertheless, her parents instructed her to read ten pages from her practice book, and then work on some division problems. She was about to heave a loud sigh when she remembered that she might get more time tonight if she wished for it.

She completed her schoolwork, as requested. She played some computer games; she put together a jigsaw puzzle; she built a two-story Lego house with a red roof, yellow-walled fence, blue walkway and green windows. Her bedtime was eight o'clock, and at seven fifteen she decided to watch a DVD movie.

"Avery, you only have thirty minutes to watch that movie. You'll have to turn it off and get ready for bed," her dad reminded her.

She was more excited than on Christmas Eve. She couldn't wait to find out if the same thing would happen: her family would get frozen in time, and she could do as she pleased. *Maybe last night was just a dream. After all, that was pretty strange. And mom and dad told me there's no such thing as magic—if it appears to be magic, then there's another reason behind it.*

She had gotten so engrossed in her movie, *The Golden Compass*, she had forgotten about time. Avery imagined herself as Lyra, and she longed for the adventures that her heroine braved.

"Avery. Bedtime. Up and at it," her dad said behind her. "You can pause your movie and pick it up where you left off."

She heaved a heavy, heavy sigh while pushing the Pause button on the DVD player remote. "I wish I had more time," she moaned, sounding more like air than voice. Suddenly it dawned on her she had made the wish—the wish for more time. She spun around to look at her dad. He was standing, still and motionless. She looked at the TV screen, and Lyra was motionless as well. "Ah. I pressed Pause," she remembered. She pressed Play, and the movie resumed where Lyra was riding Iorek Byrnison's back. She pressed Pause again, ran back to Adrian's room, and opened the door without knocking. Adrian sat at his computer, typing; his fingers were not moving. She jumped with glee, clapping her hands. She checked downstairs in her parents' office. Her mother sat with a similar glum expression, grading papers.

I think I won't be a college teacher when I grow up, Avery commented to herself.

She skipped back up the stairs, got some snacks from the pantry (which were forbidden this close to bedtime), hurried to the couch and pressed Play. She noted the time on the watch she had gotten for Christmas. "If it's the same as last night, I'll have another half hour," she whispered. "It's eight—that's eight-thirty."

She had become so engrossed in her movie, she had forgotten how fast time passes. She panicked, looking at her watch; it was almost eight-thirty. She glanced at the wall clock; it still read eight o'clock. *Seems like everything on me keeps going, while everything outside of me stops. What would happen if I wished for even more time?* she wondered. "I wish I had more time," she shouted, hurrying to get the wish in before the first one wore off.

Nothing changed. Her dad remained standing, hovering behind the couch. She pressed Play; her movie continued. Close to nine o'clock, she shouted, "I wish I had more time!" She finished *The Golden Compass*, and started watching *The Chronicles of Narnia*, diligently remembering to refresh her wish every half hour. She would have watched movies and eaten snacks all night had she not passed out on the couch from exhaustion, covered in Cheese-It crumbs.

At three in the morning her dad looked down, finding Avery asleep, sprawled on the couch.

What in the world is going on? he thought. *Am I getting senile early? I just told her to get ready for bed; now it's three in the morning, and I'm still standing here. What happened in between?* He picked her up, carried her over to the kitchen trash where he brushed the crumbs off, carried her to her bed and threw a blanket over her.

Upon exiting her bedroom, Avery's brother emerged from his room with a puzzled expression. "I'm missing more than six hours," Adrian told his dad.

Avery's mom had just come upstairs, looking perplexed. "I'm missing six hours," she said, echoing Adrian.

The three huddled outside Avery's door, completely unaware she was the cause of their confusion. They tried to figure out why each seemed to be missing six hours. At three in the morning, Avery's family members were so sleepy they could hardly stand. They were awake well past their bedtimes. Apparently, being frozen was no substitute for sleep.

Avery's alarm clock dutifully awoke her from a deep slumber; the extra time she had been granted failed to provide her with a complete night's rest. The entire family plodded through the morning's routine: showering, dressing, making the beds, preparing breakfast, brushing teeth, all in slow motion. On the trip to school, the traffic on the freeway seemed to speed by them.

Everything was back to normal at school. Avery did not remember what had happened in class the day before—she had been asleep during the entire incident, but her classmates eyed her strangely. Mrs. Zimmer was particularly vigilant of Avery's mannerisms, not wanting her to make any sleep-directed gestures whatsoever. The school day concluded normally, but with not-such-good news for Avery. Since the arithmetic exam had been cancelled the previous day for reasons Avery still did not understand, the class had to take it today. Avery was so sleepy, she made some silly errors— mistakes made only because she hadn't had enough rest.

Today was a karate day. When Avery's mom picked her up from school, she brought her karate gi—her white karate uniform with belt. Avery changed clothes in the restroom, emerging as a karate girl. Though still a white belt, she was tenacious about practicing the movements—katas. She intended to earn a black belt someday, through hard work and diligence.

The drive from school to the karate dojo was just ten minutes across town. They arrived five minutes early—five push-ups if late. Avery's mom joined the other parents in the observation area while Avery ran to join the other students. Avery's karate teacher, Sensei Yoshi, always started class on time—an extra-ordinarily punctual and precise fourth degree, black belt, karate master.

He bowed at the doorway, and then walked barefoot to the middle of the immaculate wooden dojo floor, centering himself, and facing his dutiful students. He sternly scrutinized the quality and precision of *sei ritsu*—how the students lined up, kneeling, with knees just grazing a red line marking their position. He approved, grunting in satisfaction.

"Shomen ni rei!" he shouted brusquely, the command to bow from the kneeling position—a sign of respect for the teacher, dojo and karate process.

Avery knew she excelled at this technique. Sensei Yoshi had once used her to demonstrate shomen ni rei. She kneeled, perfectly positioning her knees, placed her hands in an exact V-formation on the floor, bent squarely from her waist, and rested her head in the target formed by her hands. As her forehead touched her exquisitely placed thumbs, she heard a voice reverberating, "It's payback time, little girl...errr...Avery!"

SNORE... SNORE... SNORE... SNORE... SNORE....

Upon hearing this escalating disruption of his class, Sensei Yoshi glanced fiercely in the direction of the offender, but his disgruntled demeanor did not silence this formidable opponent. The snores meshed together, creating a resonance—

a quaking, not of the earth. The students, once perfectly in-line, were shoved against the wall behind them.

Sensei Yoshi stood his ground, maintaining the "stance of immobility." Smoke issued from under his feet from the friction against the wooden floor as the onslaught pressed him backwards. Two charred tracks marked the floor Sensei Yoshi struggled to maintain as he slid further backward. He observed—disbelievingly—Avery at the center of the commotion, though she was peaceful and still, uninterrupted in her bow of shomen ni rei, and snoring ever so loudly.

The window behind the observation group had shattered to the outside street front. Parents and observers barreled over one another and were swept out to the adjoining sidewalk. Panicked family members struggled to get back inside to rescue the children—both those pressed against the wall behind Avery, and the less fortunate pupils whipped into a whirlwind that twirled them around the room. The charred gouges made by Sensei Yoshi's feet slowly elongated in front of him; he had not forsaken his quest to save Avery. His once pristine mirrored wall dispersed into thousands of web-like cracks, as the "Do Not Touch the Mirrors" sign fluttered against his face and flew away.

By now someone had called 911. Policeman Bob and Fireman Chuck had arrived on the scene with their teams, fully armed and equipped, officiously marking their territories. Emergency units from around the county had been recruited into service as fire trucks and police cars from other communities crowded the perimeter.

Two black Suburbans with blue flashing lights drove unfettered through the havoc and took center stage. Several men in suits and dark glasses emerged. A man with a darker suit and darker glasses approached Fireman Chuck and Policeman Bob.

"This your jurisdiction?" the sun-glassed man asked, looking from one to the other. Four other sun-glassed men stood behind, their arms folded menacingly.

Policeman Bob and Fireman Chuck realized these guys were trouble—Feds here to interfere with a local problem they could handle themselves. For once, they agreed with one another. "Yes! This is OUR jurisdiction," they responded harmoniously over the ruckus one hundred feet away.

"Not anymore," the sun-glassed man replied. "This situation has become a national problem—a security threat."

"A security threat?" Fireman Chuck responded incredulously. "It's a karate class. Some children, parents and their karate instructor are in there. We don't know what's causing this disturbance, but we've got to get them out of there."

"There's one problem in there—Avery—she's a weapon of mass destruction," the federal agent replied in a monotone. "We may have to raze the entire building—possibly the block."

Fireman Chuck and Policeman Bob recoiled to the automaton-with-dark-glasses' remark, both reaching for him (to do what, they did not know), only to be pushed back by the four suits behind him.

At that instant six men dressed in desert kaki body armor, holding bazookas, took up positions in front of the building. Fireman Chuck believed he heard another man wearing sunglasses talk to an aircraft en route on a radio…something about "an air strike if the rocket launchers didn't take her out."

Sensei Yoshi brought his fifty years of training to bear, struggling against this unknown force bent upon destroying his students, his karate classroom, and the neighborhood. He glanced outside, noticing the sun-glassed men talking to Fireman Chuck and Policeman Bob, and he knew what their discussion meant: if he didn't get control of this situation, the situation would be completely out of control. He mustered his will and concentration.

Many years ago his sensei had conquered a similar foe. He had invoked a tactic little known and long forgotten. Sensei Yoshi's dad had recounted the tale to him as a boy many times. It was the ten-year-old Sensei Yoshi against whom the tactic had been invoked; it was the little Sensei Yoshi whose snores had almost destroyed a Japanese village. He had long dismissed the tale as a dream—a fantasy—of a boy who did not want to go to bed when his parents told him. But deep within the recesses of his memories, the reality survived. He recalled the voice, Vox; he remembered the false promise—the deceit: absolutely no payment unless fully satisfied. Against the maelstrom pounding against him, he searched deeply to recall his boyhood, the picture of kneeling in the dojo, his classmates flying around him. The vision of his sensei from long ago percolated to his consciousness: the tactic; the command; the motions; the kata. All must be performed clearly, harmoniously, synchronously in body and voice for the spell to be lifted: 鼾句 known as the "Loud Snoring Banishment" kata.

The rush of wind from Avery's snoring continued to push against him, edging him backward, lengthening the burned trail from his clenched feet. He dare not bend into the wind; that position would destroy the harmony—and therefore the power—of his stance. He formulated the exact method for the kata, folding his hands to his chest and bowing his head.

As Sensei Yoshi prepared to implement the complex and intricate kata, he overheard the men outside. He tried to drown out the conversation, focusing on his movement. He concentrated, forcing his vision back fifty years. From the point-of-view of his ten-year old eyes, he studied his sensei.

"Let us try tear gas first," Policeman Bob shrieked, trying to hold off a catastrophe.

The sun-glassed, suited men were ready to give the striking orders: bazookas would fire rockets, long range artillery would launch shells, and an air strike would ensue. "Certainly a few more minutes won't endanger our nation's security!" Fireman Chuck pleaded.

"We'll give you two minutes," the sun-glassed man said. "But we cannot let this situation spread. We've seen this sort of thing before; we are trained at containing this threat. Do not underestimate its power. The most devastating, apparently natural disasters in history really had children snoring at the center of them," the sun-glassed man asserted, pointing toward Avery. "That information is classified, by the way."

Sensei Yoshi knew that even the tear gas would be unacceptable, disrupting his ability to complete the complicated series of movements and gestures. He had to act immediately—and the results of his actions had to be apparent to the men outside, ready to obliterate his dojo, the neighborhood and perhaps the entire town. With no time remaining to recount the procedure, he surrendered to his inner-force—the same force that allowed him to fully visualize the circumstances of his childhood.

He leaped directly into the air, immediately rotating his body forward into the wind, forming an airfoil—a wing. He flew like a kite, an unknown string holding him in place. From an almost horizontal position, rocking slightly about a center, he jabbed and twisted, turning his hands, elbows, knees and feet. The movements were inhumanly complex, like rubbing your belly with your left hand and patting your head with your right, then switching quickly, and then switching again, over and over. Only Sensei Yoshi's movements required ten different synchronous movements, all asynchronous. Specifically placed shouts, grunts and groans were exactly interspersed with the motions. He continued this complex dance in midair for thirty seconds; stopped completely still; then spun rapidly around the axis through his head and feet. Faster and faster he spun until the energy from the snores was absorbed in Sensei Yoshi's midair turbine, like a human vacuum cleaner.

The room grew quiet. The children, who had been spinning about, slowly returned to the floor. The airborne debris settled. The force repelling the parents outside retracted, allowing them to rush inside to retrieve their sons and daughters. The sun-glassed men, looking disappointed, realized that the phenomenon had been abated. They told the men with the bazookas to drop their aim; they called off the impending air strike and told the far off artillery to fall back.

Avery still slept in her kneeling position. Her mom had rushed to her side, leaping over broken chairs and dodging other parents.

"Avery," she called, shaking her shoulders gently. "Avery, wake up," her mom said.

"Avery. It's time to get up. I prepared your favorite breakfast: waffles!" her dad announced.

Avery stirred, rolling over from her bunched position in bed. "What are these tissues doing under your pillow?" Avery's mom asked concerned, examining the tissues. "Were you crying last night? Did you have another nose bleed?"

Avery's mother's image filled her eyes. Relief poured in. Avery cried and laughed, hugging her tighter than she had ever hugged her mom before. She pulled her dad into the fray and hugged them both as hard as she could, wrapping her arms around both of them together. She didn't want to let them go.

"Avery, we woke you up a little later this morning, so you could sleep longer," Avery's dad said, "but you've got to get a move on. It's late."

She sat up in her bed momentarily, scanning her room, looking for vestiges of the night before. She ran to her closet, sliding the doors back and forth, scrutinizing the corners.

"Looking for something particular?" her mom asked. "Your school clothes are hanging where they always are," she reminded her. "And remember to get your gi. You have karate after school today."

Avery was ecstatic and did not want her mom to think she was purposefully dragging her feet and stalling for time. "Got' em," Avery replied, rattling the hangers in her closet.

As she glanced toward a corner close to her desk, she spotted it—her flashlight. "Dad, did you change the batteries in my flashlight yesterday?" Avery inquired while opening her window blinds for more light.

"Of course. You were there. Remember? I showed you how to use a volt meter," he shouted from the kitchen. "Come eat your breakfast before it gets cold."

She reached down, picked it up and switched it on. The filament glowed a very faint yellow.

Dream or real, the power to change time costs too much, and changes the things I love. They're best just the way they are.

She ate her waffles and started her day.

The Evolution

Preface

This next piece requires an explanation—a context—before proceeding. I wrote The Evolution when I was 20-21, a time of considerable developmental turmoil and strife, both for me and my collegiate cohort.

At the same time I was fascinated by the works of several stream-of-consciousness and existential writers, particularly James Joyce, William Faulkner and Fyodor Dostoevsky. My obsession with Dostoevsky was so intense I studied Russian during my first two years as a university student, thinking I could read his untranslated versions—the naiveté of youth.

This work was my first full length piece as well. Up to this time, my writing included various sappy poems and writing articles for the UCLA Daily Bruin and the Omaha Star.

Nevertheless, as I readied this piece for publication, I realized that my intended theme does percolate through— once one acclimates to the free flowing associations and stream of consciousness. A Nineteenth Century black man, whose parents were the last generation of slaves, provides the seeds for the evolution of African-Americans moving into the Twentieth Century; he provided the impetus for change. The event timeline connotes timelessness.

PREHISTORY

Cy Tyler's life passed before him as he walked alone on a bleak, frost-biting December eve. Frames of slaves in cotton fields flashed through his mind. The years fell in a cascade before him, and he laughed to himself at the thought of how simple they really were. The future seemed so far away, and yet so little time had passed. Now Cy was soon to become a father, and the strange feeling was that he really didn't care. He felt dull and numb.

He stopped at a corner and pulled up the collar of his coat. Shadows cast from the light of a gas lamp hanging above him played games upon his black skin. He stood motionless a moment, then he pulled an old cigar from his pocket and lit it. The smoke from the cigar danced and intermingled with the snow and ice slivers blown from adjacent roofs. The black shadows and the white snow seemed strangely merged into a queer oneness that saturated the atmosphere.

Up and down the street the red lights were twinkling in the prostitute houses. This was Cy's neighborhood. On several occasions Cy was tempted to go into one of those places, but he always thought of his wife at home, awaiting him. Tonight he was tempted, and his wife was at home, nearly nine months into pregnancy. The thought of what color the baby would be amused him; he grinned.

He stepped into the street and walked across the slippery, slush-covered bricks to the door of the house with the red light. He knocked---knocked as if he didn't want anyone to hear him, but he wanted someone to answer. He noticed his shadow cast on the door before him—a distorted shadow, giving his body the appearance of a toy top. The knees of the shadow were bent at the angle between the door and the ground. He heard several footsteps beyond the door, a latch fall and a lock click. When the door opened, he was confronted with a half-naked, wild-haired woman with heavy make-up smeared on her face. A stench of opium, cigarette smoke, vomit, and sex burst from the door. The smell trickled up his nose, and he marveled at it, and shivered. The woman stood before him, arms folded, with an expectant and irritated expression.

"Well, come on in! I don't wanna stand in the goddam door all night!"

One frame of his mother flowed lighting fast into and out his of mind---then another frame of a vague farm scene. *o, to be a child again, and i forgot beauty, and my mother, and the hay in the field that the cows can eat, but i can't, except for when no one is looking, besides the cows, but they never say grace at the table, so how are they to judge what is good, but they don't, because they remain in the fields all their lives, and shit on the cool moist ground that i'm not supposed to lie in, because i'll get dirty, and fuel is hard to come by to take a hot bath, because we say grace at the table, because we are children, and we might get dirty, but don't they know that shit burns?*

"Hey mista, what you gonna do? Is you gonna come in, or is you gonna stay out?"

Cy walked away.

"Crazy muthafuka," she murmered as she slammed the door.

He tossed the cigar aside. It bounced, spraying sparks and rolled into the gutter.

The distant bell in the post office tower echoed eleven times. When it stopped, he heard no other sound but his own. The crunch of his footsteps upon the ice took up a steady cadence, and the silence of the street seemed to bellow out against its intruder. A Jewish pawnshop proprietor appeared in an opened door, and they conversed. *in the beginning God created the heaven and earth, and the earth was without frame, and void, and darkness was upon the face of the deep, and the spirit of God moved upon the face of the waters, until the seventh day when someone rolled seven and crapped out, and it was good to finally see the light of day and the darkness of night, even though it was so short lived, but i want to be immortal, and i don't know how, and this man claims he knows, and the man down the street claims he knows, and if there were only someone who really knew, because there are*

97

too many gods who claim to be god, but God is resting, and he hears our pleas, but they are not of God, and even God has senses, and god cannot communicate, because he is listening to this Jew, and the Chinese who has a laundry down the street, and they are religious, and i am not, and i am a wretched sinner who basks in the flowers of day, and the cool breezes of night, and i don't eat apples because i might start going to church o God please help me to be like you.

And so the old Jew finished his story of how his wife killed herself by chopping off her hand with a cleaver, eating her own hand in a fit of madness, and then consequently, contracting gangrene. Cy thanked the old man, and continued.

The small, squalor, dingy buildings passed him more rapidly. Off in the distance he saw the dark form of the bridge crossing the M. River. A young wino barred his path, stopping him with tears in his eyes. He looked slowly toward the river, and then back to Cy, muttering some jarbled words Cy thought was madness.

"...but the two sides of a river really aren't separated. There is only a separation in the means of travel from one bank to another, and that's why there are bridges---to maintain a constant..."

But Cy ignored the man, and pushed on.

At the corner Cy turned off 12th Street onto D. Street, cutting the corner as a soldier would make a column movement. Occasionally, a gust of wind would blow up against him, and he smiled.

Suddenly, his heart began to beat wildly. Droplets of sweat formed on his forehead, his hands and in his armpits. He stopped at the door of a run-down, unpainted two story building. The building had a restaurant on the first floor and some rented rooms on the second floor. Painted on the large, plate glass window of the restaurant was "Little Arkansas." The window reflected the sign on the missionary window across the street--Jesus Saves.

Cy raised his hand slowly, and grasped the door knob. *men are proud, nervous, eager, happy, elated, depressed, and satisfied when wife begets child, but i am guilty of a crime committed against*

god's nature of things, and so i suffer under the
table upon which my family is saying grace, and
they kick me under the table, and throw me the
crumbs of bread and wine, when i would prefer the
cow shit of the meadow to what i am starved at the
alter, and so i commit the most unnatural deed of
all, which is to fuck my father in my mother's
presence, and my brothers and sisters laugh
because i love an unnatural woman reserved only
for god, because God cursed her, and her husband
eons ago, as i now am now to witness the execution
of my half-breed son, and it will be a son so that my
labor pains will be twelve-fold that of a daughter
who undergoes the same pain as the serpent on the
tree, but alas, all and no hope vanishes if the boy
lives, for he will also nurse the labor pains, and
God knows what he will create, and now i have died
in the earth that i have loved and hated for so short
a time.

The distant bell in the post office tower
echoed twelve times. As the bell tolled for the

twelfth time, the wail of a baby emerged from beyond the door.

EXISTENCE

if i were to be a doctor, who could i heal so
that i might save myself from heaven and hell, so
that my black father might follow me in my return
to nonconception, but if i die, all things to be will
exist no more, and there will be no more children of
israel, except in story books that are read as bedtime
stories in prostitute houses, by which all may be
perplexed, because they want to watch television in
1891, whereas i prefer to play with my genital
organ, and smell up my hands with the foul smell of
lilacs on the mount-of ocean fishermen, where
bluegills are returned to the water, only to have
breathed the stench of air once, or be fried in a
skillet at some priest's place of business, where nuns
are the gardeners, and dead jack-o-lanterns for
yesterdays halloweens are raised, because there is
no christmas to look forward to, but only a holiday
when the football players are paid off for fucking
the nuns who are out in the garden, but alas, i now
empirically be, whereas i was part of my family
before, and this was not meant to be, and it is sinful

for me to eat of the fruit, but this woman is stronger than i, and she is forcing it into my navel, and so, i am stagnant, for i have died before i have ever tasted the fruits of life. how i long for God to caress my testes once more, so that i may again be a Man, but hence, i have long lost my awareness of God in but an instant of excretion, but i have gained affection for the aroma of this woman's vagina, and to both of them i shall return to bathe myself with lye, and again let the harsh, pulsating waves emulsify me, make me erect, and give me new life, so that i may die a birth of joy that is felt only when i climb ropes, and define myself to a life of blessed quality and infinite quantity, stretching to the finest of loves and the finest of hates. and now they wash the water off me only to baptize me.

     into an existence of applesauce and muck, and if my father were only aware of my pride in him for basking in the flowers of day and the cool breezes of night, and wallowing in shit, and scraping it off his body to build a fire for a hot bath in a witch's cauldron, and masturbating God in god's presence and unawareness, only to master the highest social knowledge possible, simply to keep nuns virgins, and priests pimps, and caress the thighs of the mothers who don't bare children, but clothe them to protect them from their own searching hands, and i know of all the forbearers who have worked to make the coming possible, simply so that i may sit at ease until i know her once more, my beautiful mother, God-mother, and great-grandmother of Cain's noble and wretched mistress of God.

ii

and i peer into the windows of the temple, only to see the carcasses of empty wine bottles piled up against the door, allowing no one exit nor entrance, and the dregs greased upon the already frictionless floor, causing heat. and i heard a noise outside, and it was a baby crying, and i stopped to listen, but the applause within the temple was overwhelming, except for the tears of my father, which fell to the floor and neutralized the acidity of the wine dregs, and i partook of the feast within the undercroft, and i vomited, and vowed to remain in a corner, only to weep the tears of my mother's natural oils, but i would not drop to my knees to pray even though becoming overwhelmed by the drug, and i found the drug was self-perpetuating, and it amputated my arms to the pits so i could not hide my eyes, nor cover my ears, nor my mouth, and though i remained in the corner, i was goaded into an act of a self-righteous clown who humiliated me by laughing, and i watched the temple lick up dead sperm, and grow, whilst i await the second octave. and i am stripped of my clothing by an old woman who wants me to rape her, and she disrobes me, only to find i am wearing no underwear, at which she is mortified, and she sucks my fertile and buxom breasts until they are barren, and leaves me to live with inaccessible sexuality, and i am relieved by the mildness of purgatory.

iii

and i ride with a calvary of officers, and i shoot off privates for being foot soldiers, but i am cramped against this saddle of rivets and bone, so that my Manhood is squeezed and caressed out of me by engineers who build bridges, and destroy rivers, and allow fecal matter and shit to flow freely under the street to clog up traffic. and if i were a carpenter, i would build the finest buildings that the engineers would copy, and resell at bargain prices in the cellar of the black market, where i shall hang with severed loins and limbs, price-tagged, and put up for display in the window so that passers-by may sneer and marvel at how well the carving was done, and they nod their silly heads with approval, and go home, and prostitute their children, and commit incest with their mothers, so that father can have his penis hard, and masturbate, and clean up the mess with used toilet paper, and they go to church seven days a day, and watch the minister pick his nose, and flick the coagulations at the cross, and put the cross on the steeple for a congregation of brides to wretch upon, and guide ships to india, where the cattle are men, and the men are men, and the anthropologists shake their heads with disapproval, and congratulate themselves for the castration of a woman who is mary, but there is the slightest recollection of a Mary in me, but the nostalgia is weakening rapidly, and I am isolated and alone with only a peephole that is exponentially growing smaller.

iv

and in the back bone of every man there are vertebrae that are the source of all jewelry and species, and they kick one another, and shoot and kill and maim, and call home to the wife and kids to tell them that you are out with some whore tonight, and that you will not be home to eat chitterlings and wild rice, but that you will send the singing postman to your front door with a gun so that he can kill the family dog that you have invested so much time and money into, simply so that your kids can take the fire hydrants to school that it pisses upon, and give them to teacher, and she decapitated your children to demonstrate the french revolution, and all the other children are overcome by such a magnanimous act of mercy, and they all mob to your lawn, and burn niggers and buddist monks, and throw them down your chimney to smoke out the storks, and you hang the nigger above the fireplace, and paint the remains of the monk red, and you watch the nigger closely, so that he won't kiss you while you are asleep, for what an abomination it would be to have black lips, for the doctor bill for the amputation would be enormous, but a very small amount to the professor who holds the lips in a jar of formaldehyde, only to put them to his mouth in lust for his mother, who never bore you nor him, but how are you to understand me if all you do is pole-vault, and eat popcorn that is unseasoned and crusted with ringworm, so that you contract a cancerous case of venereal disease that permeates your body, and kills scabies mites on contact, just as mercury determines the temperature of a thermometer in a football pen.

and it is surprising that newton would begin under an apple tree, and later be a rich man with his

own little dancing troupe on the moon, all of them
running around playing lyres and harps, and since
they cannot breathe, they think that they are in
heaven, when Heaven is within them, but then
newton was supposed to tell them all about the lack
of oxygen on the moon, so that is why you see a
face if you breathe and smell with your nose, but
maybe you should donate yourself as the family
dog, so that you, too, can have wild whooping crane
every fourth of july and passover, and it will be
interesting to breed the kind of sterile fleas that you
collect while tipping the lifeguard at the beach, and
if at any time you should decide to become a
fortune teller, you can depend on me for telling your
fortune, for i shall kill you by not dying with you,
but you will find your way among the dead, and i
shall seek out the living.

v

so here i am as an alter boy, singing praises
to god, and attending church services with Jews
who sit in the back pews and eat ham, whereas i fill
the censor with marihuana and opium poppies, only

109

awaiting the coming of the amphetamines, so that i may escape the forlorn of escaping, but there is another route, and that is through the labyrinth and maze of tunnels that complicate the cellar of a certain frequented prison.

0 Father who art in Heaven, hallowed be thy Name, Thy Kingdom come, Thy Will be done on earth as it is in Heaven. Give us this day our daily bread and forgive us our trespasses as we forgive those who trespass against us, and lead us not into temptation, but deliver us from evil, for Thine is the kingdom and the power and the glory forever and ever. and now they are choking me for refusing to say amen, but I will never say amen.

vi

It was a bleak, mucky, hot summer day. The funeral chapel was air conditioned, and the people filed out with half grievous, half imposed-upon looks.

The funeral procession was organized, and it proceeded along soft, black-top streets to the cemetery. There it came to a shady nook of trees, where it planted it's dead seed into the ground. Like stupid, ruddy sharecroppers who don't know what to let live when its alive, let alone what to plant after it dies, they went about their gardening duties.

And they stand about and go through their pagan ceremony, cross themselves, and take leave, just to go home and gossip of the doctor's funeral, like it was a public exhibition.

The shiny, silvery casket sparkles and glimmers with sprinkles of sunlight through the rustling leaves of the trees that surround it. The day is blue and clear. A drop of water falls on the cold metal surface, beads up and rolls off.

CONCEPTION

i

and with all the love and kindness that a
mother can give to her child, i now thrash open your
hymen so that you too, can give birth to chordata,
and feed in the flowing, fertile, fragrant fields of
wheat, and thus hunt wild animals while shunning
the staple appetite that struggles so urgently to be
used by your fingers and your toes. and if i were a
virgin, as you will be, i would call all men from afar
to behold my wicked sinfulness as i cringe in the
hay, and dodge the teeth of cows and horses as they
snap and bite at one another to emulsify their
canines in the frost of my blue blood, but i am not
perplexed, for my father and mother were both
damned, as myself, and therefore, i feel neither
alone nor hurt. and with my hands and my feet i can
grope more freely, avoiding the dangers, while still
unable to heed the signs that beckon me onward, up
the rocky slopes. and the mountain breezes caress
me gently, and lubricate me, so that if i should slip,
i will fall with speed and grace, passing the most

peaceful of birds that continues to search for its
maiden ship, from which it was sent to plant olive
trees in muck that has yet to dry, but the muck will
ease my impact, and the bird cannot light to plant its
tree.

     and now i stand at the glory pits of doom,
with my hands on my breasts and thighs, marveling
at the horizon of the sky as it nestles to the bountiful
earth below, and she kissed him softly and let the
lava of the under-earth and the balmy nothingness
above flow from his mind to her pineal, where all
worlds meet, and the Glories that are Our's and
Heaven's within and about bless it. and in the
wakening hours of dawn, i kiss her sweet lips
gently, and i tell her to sigh as if in oblivion, and
she obeys, and vomits blood, and she goes about her
dolls and counts them, and cries because they do not
want to play with her because of their number, and
she burns all but one, and that one she keeps and
cherishes and admires, as if it were her own, but the
doll is impervious to her whims and affections and
casts an evil eye at her and spits, and breaks her

113

heart. and she spanks the doll and places it in the corner as punishment, and she goes to play with mommy instead, who is in the kitchen baking and sewing and cleaning and fucking, and she looks on as mommy goes about her chores, and she wonders whether mommy is sick because she is crying, and her mother notices her daughter's attentiveness, and she curses her and demands that she leave the room immediately, because she has not yet reached puberty, so how is she to know what is right and what is wrong for her to smell and taste and see and feel and hear, and the little girl obeys her mother and falls to her knees and prays, and sings hymns, and begs for forgiveness of her sins so that some day she too may be baptized into puberty.

 and a deluge of books fall onto the male moles of the sea, and they develop antlers so that they might breathe, but they find that the ocean water is impure, and so they emerge onto isles of darkness and disregard their antlers to the impure water, and they breed virus, and make it well, so that they flourish to sneeze and gag and cough, and they walk and run and fly and climb and swing and build and multiply, but they never return to their once betrothed, impure sea water, where life was clean and fresh, and where colors were known, and not sensed, and the artists were scientists, and the scientists were prophets, and the prophets were beggars, and beggars knew All and had nothing.

and he is dreaming of fishermen plunging their nets onto the sea shore and carrying the sand in their nets to glass factories, and the chimneys of the factories belch out fire and water and oxygen and nitrogen, and the surrounding fishing villages pur-chase the glass and build boats, and the pregnant wives of the fishermen venture out into the treacherous waters to save dying seamen from the misery of dying for their country, and a violent storm dashes the boats and the wives and the seamen to the shore where ages pass, and once again the fishermen come to cast their nets onto the shore and carry the sand to the factories, but one fisherman out of all the rest wonders why the glass factory is not itself built of glass, but is constructed

115

of sand, so he builds a boat of sand, and he sails into the friendly waters, and casts his net, but catches nothing, so he sails for days and days, hoping sometime to come to the end of his journey, and he notices that the chimneys of the factories are never out of his sight; that they seem to be watching him to protect themselves from him and his tiny boat of sand, and he wonders why there is no end to the waters, so he cannot catch fish, and after much deliberation, he discovers that the sea is a mote around the factories, and the mote is made of glass, and he looks over the edge of his tiny vessel to see his reflection in the glass sea, and it is clear and perfect in every detail, but he has never seen his reflection before , and come night fall, his reflection slowly disappears with the setting sun, but during the night, a meteor fell, and broke the glass, and the water underneath rushes up and melts the fisherman and his boat, and the factories look on silently.

i stand invisible in a room of darkness, groping for reflections and shadows, and i hap upon a mirror of another room to the right and to the left and up and down and in the center and, oh, stop, i am in a frenzy trying to get a glimpse of the shadows of the room in the mirror, for it moves with calculated inconsistency, and i am neither prepared nor willing nor living to cross its threshold, for if i should, even for an instant, become part, i would be cast into all directions, illuminating men, and destroying all that i have died for, and so i struggle for escape and i am caught up by some moveable form that penetrates my pupils so that the shadows of the mirror light my face. i see a dining room, and a wall of mirrors reflecting and divining, and they ebb and flow in directionless shuffling, and then, my pupils, as if the power were optically innate, adjust, and in only my eyes, the images integrate themselves, so that I can distinguish smoke, emanating from some source off to a side of the mirror, but not in the range of projection. and the smoke is exhaled and inhaled, never allowed to

117

diffuse into the air, as if the smoke were a large water droplet at the end of a bellows, being sucked in, and being blown out, and the smoke has a thin, translucent haze around it, and it glows at each new breath of life, so that it never really lives nor dies, but simply vibrates in innumerable sizes, locations and velocities. and i peer into the smoke droplet closely, and i see stars and suns and galaxies and planets and earth and water, and the vastness of god in some simple rocks and crustations. and peering over one of the crustations i see a man in an asbestos suit, with tanks on his back, and i wonder if he is an explorer or a fire fighter, for if he is an explorer, he may discover what heat lies within the crustation, but if he is a fire fighter he will merely sacrifice himself unknowingly to the sun gods that await him. and through the eyes of the asbestos man, i witness explosions on the sun. my curiosity writhes and my pupils expand and enlarge, so that now giant quasar systems come into view, and they flash by my eyesight one by one, enumerated so that i may count, but as the pace hastens, the numbers become unintelligible, and the blue is an amoeba, and so, along with the man in asbestos, i delve into the cell and i find myself immersed in acid that soothes rather than corrodes, and i swim into the depths of this acid-sea, and i discover spiraling rocks, and their surfaces are smooth and adhering, so that i board the top of one, and slide down, gliding with the loops until i enter a spherical labyrinth where the surface ceases to conduct me. and i look about me for more spirals, but i see only a multitude of pendulums and bouncing balls of indefinable magnitudes, numbers and directions for as close and as far as my eyes can delve. and the incessant motion bewilders me, for i cannot follow a single ball or pendulum in its harmonic motion, and i realize that each globe is visible at the start and finish and finish and start of its vibration. and in my searching wonderment, i have not stopped even to notice what supports me, and i hang my head and gaze into a mirrored floor, and i am startled at the reappearance of the same bellowed smoke droplet, but i do now distinguish a dark round formation in the reflecting, shadowing glass, and i peer into darkness and i see a face, a woman's face, and i perceive that it is mine, and i reach for it, and i stretch my arm and my hand and my fingers until the joints nearly pop, and the face beckons me, and lures me into the living abyss, and i float and fall helplessly, and i can't yell, but i must, yet i know that if i do, i will again no longer conceive and desire what is mine, but my eyes bulge, and my mind is unaccustomed to such light, and i yell— why?—and i reappear as a virgin, copulating with my husband, and i have lost my entire motion of existence.

ii

and so to thee, my mother of god, i bless thee and give thee all the comfort and love that a heart and soul might give, but where in our wakening hours when we no longer are frightened by the winds that set the sails of mills to flight that we might fly with them and sow the grains of the field and fertilize the soils of the sea with nutriments from our bodies, but only until then, can

we ever hope to prosper into an existence that

allows us to grow within our means, where our

children are your children, and we all live

under the same flag of state, and soldiers will

fight not for flags and gods and wives and honor

and power and the shit and sweat that permeate and

foul our very existence, so that all essential qualities

of you and i are sifted and burned in a well of

stagnated sewer rot where little men and women

with pen and paper come to dictate how their slop is

to be cleaned up for urban renewal, and new wells

are built for more refined and sophisticated sewer

rot with a similar stench, only medicated to keep us

from escaping or complaining, and is cheaper and

easier to prepare, so that some of the drudgeries are

taken out of life, and everyone can smell and taste

the stench of the sewers more cheaply and easily, so

that even the lowliest business man and farmer on

the street might benefit from the progress of our rich

and highly cultured society called man. and so

hence forward i thrust my self into the dark and

gloomy smoke-infested gullies of the night, where the odor of dead organic matter runs in rivers, and floods the valleys that have just passed smog prevention laws, so that now the towns folk are riled, and they search the gullies with gas masks and flash lights, and i creep in and out of the crevices and dodge the lights as they pass in my direction, and i reach the end of the gully and i plunge head-long into a river once used to fertilize the valley of the town's people, but they have become too busy with their silly laws and gas masks, so now the river offers for me a means of escape and revitalization, so that with each stroke of my arm, i feel younger and more alive and even more willing to accept my role at the bottom of the river as a water-logged corpse.

so walk along the edge of hell and see where it gets you, you sniveling fool of the post-was era of mozart and locke, but because you walk that thin line, i am kept in a constant state of amusement, always knowing where my next meal arises, and while i digest, i lay back with my arms crossed and

dream of paganistic rituals of grueling gore and
shining horror, where young female babes are
emasculated and changed to male mosquitoes that
don't know their own species, and woo fleas and
chickens in the daylight of the quarter moon, and
they play the buffoons of the insect world and
collect pollen from cone trees and bite the bears for
stealing their honey, and the bears roar and growl
and attack campers in a near-by rest resort, and the
park officials are infuriated, and they take out their
pistols and guns and search for the rejected and
hostile bears, but the bears are not to be found, for
they were rewarded for their noble act of relieving
woman of her bikini, and skinning her, and coating
her with feathers and honey and throwing her in the
outside oversized bath tub that is infested with the
murk and filth of polluted swimming trunks. and I
swim in a school of luminescent fish, each fish
having all the colors and sounds of the spectrum,
and they display them for me, and impress me with
the brightness of day and the blackness of night, and
they see that I am impressed, and so they invite me

to join them, and we swim and dive and circle about through cool green and blue waters made present only by the natural wonders of these streamlined creatures of the underworld. and i ask one fish, But truly, you must have a destination? and i am soon to discover that the destination is a natural curse, and that once it is reached, the fish die, and along with them, all the life of atlantis becomes flooded with the life and rotten breath of some foreign creature meant to destroy itself by ex-panding into balloon-like existence.

and in my shining hour i shall blossom forth from a thousand different flowers of plastic and metal fields rich in mineral resources, but untouched by neither man nor woman alike, where all our most fanciful and stifled thoughts flee to escape conviction by a nonsectarian judge who is impotent and has been teased and harassed by his wife for thirty years, but in the softness of his masculinity they did conceive one off-spring that spends its time reveling in its own reluctant creation, wondering why he is not recognized as the leader of the tribe by his kinsmen, until someone murders the young man by informing him that he is nothing, and he has no kinsmen like the man on tv says and he shuffles away, rubbing acne medicine into his skin, and wallowing in the muck of his own self-pity, still unwilling to admit that his seeds are just as dead as the rest, and argues that his acne has disappeared.

DICHOTOMY

the twin siamese babies of the womb are formed in complete wholeness; the opposite poles of the earth work to crush and maintain us; for every action there is an equal and opposite reaction; without light, there is darkness; without darkness, there is light; every person is a unique individual, even though he has certain opposing traits in his personality which form dynamic tensions; an eye for an eye, a tooth for a tooth; many biological organisms are bilateral.

the whole of the Universe exists within a certain locus of beach upon which the swimmer swims, and the bather bathes, and each can say that this is the beach, but until each one can say we are one man, will the trueness of time and morality be a ripe and fertile concept in the mind of man, and he will run to the beach in full strides, and examine the sea and the water, and the waves, and the tides with complete pride and dignity, and he will frolically challenge the dynamic waves of force to a duel, and laugh in the midst of the shock, so that now he shall be dashed to the sands to land softly and comfortably in a bed that has never been slept in, but over which feet have trampled from the beginnings of evolution and creation.

so in the darkness of night shall the wormy, slimy grunion crawl over the fertile sands from the filthy depths of the sea to plant their destructive eggs in the sand, for afterwards the eggs hatch, and out crawl all the distinguished ideas, hopes, plans, concepts, ambitions, potentials, aspirations, and discoveries of all my people from their beginning to the end, and all the trustees, with their grins on each face, run up to you and shake your hand in desperation of leaving your company, so that you ask, why should he shake my hand at all if he's in a hurry? and furthermore, for where is he in a hurry? and if he gives me an answer, who gave it to him? and if someone gave it to him, then god help him, for he was strong enough fool to maintain it. so I sit in the corner on the curb and amuse myself with the antics of you and the trustees, when miraculously you thrust yourself from the encirclement, and fly from your and my beloved beach, and the trustees become perturbed, and declare war upon the beach, and they run off, and scurry back with their weapons, and begin bombarding the beach, and they urinate on the weapons to cool them, and they continue the onslaught, destroying the beach, and in so doing, destroyed their posterity and own place of birth.

Reflection

he stares closely at the portrait on the wall---
the face that is so enticing, and so repulsive; so
tense, and so relaxed; so invigorating, and so
depressing; so pungent, yet so dull; so loveable, yet
he'd like to rip it off the wall, caress it, and kill it,
but he glares at it, and it hangs on the wall,
depicting all that he would like to be himself, but he
is not allowed to be by the high command, who
would instantly put him under arrest for
rehabilitation if they knew that he possessed the
painting, and that he was thinking with it, but what
he doesn't know is what the picture is telling him,
that he will only lead a double life by thinking about
it, so why must he defy the laws of his species,
when they love him, and wish to help him, but he
prefers the fantasy forecasted in the face on the
wall, and he gets high, and examines the soft stone
face, line by line, crevice by crevice, texture by
texture, until tears flow from his eyes, and he is
engulfed in an overpowering drive to know and
understand and be part of the universe as the face

prescribes to him, and he learns that only from the ambivalence of the face can he be free to master time and space as he was created, to approach that nondimensional asymptote that is yet to be known, to spread his arms and legs in the blasting heat of the stars and yell in excruciating pleasure that he is now a Man fulfilling his own Will and Volition in the function of fate. and the eyes of the figure, so intense and so lethargic; so sad and so gay; so sinister and so benevolent, that as he looked deeper he was distorted into another dimension of logic and reality, and he plunged into it head-long, relinquishing himself from time and space, and became God-like, and in this cloudy enigma, he had control over concepts and forms and all corporeal things in his perceptual field, and he ruled; distance became nonexistent to him, for he knew nothing of time; reality became nonexistent to him, for he knew nothing of space; he had another Reality, and with it he could see over the entire universe to the boundaries of the next, but to this he knew that the boundaries were of him, and not of Reality of the

130

Universe; he must continue his process along the asymptotic function if his species is to evolve. to this, emissaries from the high command tried to stop him , but he was too far gone, and he disappeared from their view.

the portrait was destroyed along with the rest.

Sensation

oh, the feeling was ecstatic. she had taken it into her body, and now she was etherized into a world of sorrow and shame, and bliss and paradise, and she moved in and out room after room, color after color, sound after sound, though the corridor down which she could see for miles and miles, and upon each door was a geometric inscription, and each one fascinated her, and played games with her wandering mind, for they all were meaningful to her, and she could not discern the meaning, and she looked back, and she saw a head of her, and she turned round and around in cruel defiance of the social trend of religion, and she could see neither here nor there, but she had to have entered somewhere within the infinite barrage of exits. and she was levitated, and she flew with no speed at all through the abysmal tunnel, and as she flew, she was struck with the shocking realities that she had died to see, and the stroboscopic spectrum flashed at her in time intervals so long and so short that no swiss time master's clock could conceive of registering them to the massive crowd that awaits below the balcony to be lifted from their confusion of chaos. and she glides through the tunnel feeling no motion, nor time, nor love, nor hate, nor desire, but she moves along a path beyond infinity, and approaches the oneness of nondimensionality, and she wonders what perspective the teeming crowd below considers her, for she discovers, as she has known all along, that it is the crowd, just as well as herself, that determines her fate, for where one man is high, and the other is set, no ends can be attained. and the colors and sounds vibrate in directionless unity, and the multitude of doers and passages persist with polarity and magnetism to one door, and it drew her toward itself, and all the struggling and apathy that she could conjure up would be useless to her, for she had an affinity to the door, and she was blasted through the porthole into the open air, where the hoards of angry people snatched her up, and hailed her as a hero, then nailed her to a cross to be crucified in her own repugnance.

and as i stroll along softly in the prairie, thinking and reflecting, and introspecting, and all the other things i do to assist them in enslaving me, i meet a wall of tall grass and shrub growth, and i push aside the tall grass until i reach an isthmus clearing made by the surrounding vegetation, and i enter the clearing that is interrupted to the west by a cliff whose rocky slopes drop some hundreds of feet to a jagged beach below, and i sit, cross-legged in the middle of the clearing, and peer out over the cliff at the ships and boats at sea. and i focus my attention on one sailboat, alone in the waters, with only the sun above it, and i think that though the ocean and mountain breezes feel soothing to me, they are also giving power to the tiny vessel, and to the people on the boat. this is good, for they are pushed along, and they know it, and feel it, whereas, to me, i am neither in the boat, nor do i hear the rustling of sails, nor the rippling and splashing of the waves, nor the conversation of the people, nor can i see myself through binoculars as a tiny black dot atop a rocky cliff on the side of this mountain, but i do feel the breeze itself, and this feeling alone allows me passage, so that if all things were right, i could fly down and be on the sailboat, and feel all those things that i should be able to sense at once, but which the people in the boat won't allow me. so I satisfy myself in watching what goes on below, only to see a diver slowly emerging from the shallow surf, and carrying with him a half fleshed skull, which he throws to the sand, and he runs out the water, and falls weeping in front the skull, and bows in fits of crying, hunched contortions, and he reaches out and gently takes the skull in his hands, and he places its mouth to his lips, and he kisses it violently, as if in heat, and he rolls, and tosses, and reaches, and grabs, and moans, and turns in the sand with the skull pressed tightly to his lips, and a crowd develops, and stands about watching him, until an ambulance comes and takes him away, and i think, "they didn't catch me."

I

"Who are you, and what is your purpose for being here?"

"I am; my purpose is to be."

"Then why have you come to this locus of space, for all the existence here is in a continuous and fused state of flux, so that how can you find yourself in a space where you are not?"

"i merely look around in a manner in which you are not acquainted, for, what you do not see is that any time or space is at one time or space, or the other, and since i am—seeking to be—I merely am all times and spaces that I am, thus, to be me, and to be me is I, whose limit is I approaching I. and though you see one of me, which is a one of you, I see one and all of you, and, hence, I know where I am yesterday, today and tomorrow. but todays and tomorrows are only line existent, and so in the geometry of your world, I am not only non-being, but also nonexistent. now try to conceive of linear existence."

"I know that linear existence is not to the level or rank of existence that two and three dimentional existence has achieved, and that linear existence is only one direction, while planar and solid dimentions have two and three directions, respectively. and besides, only we three dimentionals can have corporeal existence, which we are extremely proud of, and will become nonexistent to maintain, or even advance it."

"But have you ever conceived of point-being?"

"Point? What is a point?"

"A point is the only one and it is all."

"But what about lines, and plances, and solids, and curves?"

"They are of a point, as is all, but they are not all---nor is their media of self-perpetuation of spirit all-seeking."

"You speak in nonsense terms and phrases. you are incommunicable; therefore, you are one of the ignorant ones. why have you left your cubicle?"

"Ah. so i see your locus has also found that which is known to you as 'forbade'. you have a 'culture' stamped upon your chemical minds which is your media for perpetuation. this culture, which has many sub-cultures existing in your present and history, has value as its medium of perpetuation. all your thought processes ride atop your brows, upon each stamped 'values'. each individual in your culture is a self-regulated system of rules, spawned out of a thing you call a society—yours is the society called man. a society, in turn, is a group of these individuals uniting to maintain a common set of rules upon which all actions are prescribed—value being the sole set and denominator. you even have a book which describes your sins to you, but you reject it by cancerizing your members with ignorance, contradiction, and folly, leaving them in helpless and disgusting satisfaction with your and their sinful nature."

"Ha! You speak of sin, incommunicable one, but just how can you define a sin?"

"The question should be, 'how do you define sine?' for in Reality, i know nothing of sin. it is a fantasy, a fiction, and i cannot tell you of it."

"But you used the word in context."

"I used the word in a context that you perceive."

"Then why not give me a definition in a context that i perceive?"

"Because i know of many, and all, and there is only one that you can know."

"Then tell me that one."

I am unable to."

"Why?"

"Because that one is of all, and nothing is really separable."

"Ha! Go on now, incommunicable one. go back to your cubicle before i go kill your mother."

"But you speak to one not of your locus. i shall fade from your perception, but before i do, i give to you the blessing and curse of my destination, which is now yours, and is presently how you perceive it."

She disappeared.

***

"Sir, you have been tried and convicted for a grave and serious crime against man and his kind. You have been convicted of premeditated, predestined, predetermined, or blundered 'being what-you-are-not' in the first degree. Do you have anything to say for your grave and serious crime before i sentence you to be executed?"

"No sir, your honorable one."

"Your honor!"

"Yes sir."

"Yes sir, what?!"

"Your honor."

"I sentence you to be put to death by any method the royal cook sees fit."

"Objection, your honor."

"Objections, Defense? You can't object a sentence. As a matter of fact, in this particular trial, you can't appeal it; you cannot defend it. Now, sit down, my boy, and behave yourself before i hold you with contempt. Does Prosecution have anything to say, now that Defense is silent?"

"No, your honor, except for the fact that i am held in total relief for the good of the state, that this man is convicted, and shall be put to death. But, begging your honor's pardon, is not the man's sentence exactly that which he wishes to be—what he is not? And he certainly is not dead. Yet the converse, br'nging him back to life after he has died, would seem to him a death, though, to us it would seem a great accomplishment. I also think that in the matter of this particular person no accomplishment is too great, due to the magnitude of the crime, and the man's unprecedented ability to enact it."

"Excellent point, Mr. Prosecutor. Well spoken. I'll change my sentence immediately."

The judge faces the convicted man, and clears his throat.

"Sir, you are resentenced to be put to death in a manner such that it is conducive to your being brought back to life. You shall then be brought back to life, and allowed to go freely."

Comments from an Objectionable Observer, after the trial:

Hi! I'm an Objectionable Observer, and I'd like to make a comment. Life after death is better than death after life, since all we know about death is that it is a logical negation of life—so, think positively, folks! (A crowd's muffled laughter emerges from somewhere.)

Two more Objectionable Observers: (both sitting across a plain, white, enamel, fucked-up kitchen table. An ash tray is between them, and they are passing a joint. Man who first speaks has just taken a drag).

"Wha'd you think of that trial?"

"It definitely bagged me out. The Man was talking some heavy shit."

"I don't know, man. Every time I smoke weed, I get to think'n."

"Yeah. I know what you mean. I do that thing occasionally, myself. Tell me, so we can both trip together."

"Well, it seems to me that the man who was convicted get squared up. I mean, why kill the dude if you're going to bring him back to life, anyway? It don't make sense."

"None of that heavy shit makes sense to me."

"It doesn't to me, either, but it just seems funny, that's all. Funny as hell.

II

the sound pierced his ears in a myriad of
torturous directions, all of them tormenting him
with their uniqueness, yet all of them being of the
same nature, so as to diffract at the instant of being
pursued, but if all directions were cast away, then as
she flies into the horizon, all the varieties of lights
flood her with a being that she had never before
conceived, and even radio signals and rays from
outer space had a special significance to her, and
even the trees and flames were of her, and she
smiled, for all the universe smiled upon her, for she
finally beheld her mother in her totality, but she was
nothing like she expected, since she had been told
that to meditate on Sunday was wrong, so when
would she see her parent if six days out of the week
she boards at a dump of painted faces and bodies
that force themselves into her bedroom, where they
sit opposite and goggle at one another, and where
she is taught the lesson of the day, until she goes to
sleep and reviews them in her dreams at night.

and then you tell me that she is a fine, upstanding girl, who would make a good mate for me, who would cook, and sew, and raise my children, and stick them in rancid church pews, where they should grow up and be like you, or her, or that painted face there on the stage, or screen, or pulpit. you mean, you want my son to carry your and my name, yet still spawn the same type of existence that has frustrated both you and me? you ask me to bring a saboteur of our beings into our realm of existence, and allow her to have control over our already damaged domain? this pure virgin of a woman, you say, who is told she is great, and hence, she is great? and because of that glowing rat trap, or that box of singing nonsense syllables, or that page of warped language and appeals for you to come buy a car, or smoke cigarette, or smell different from how you already smell, they are the sole contributors to your already funky disposition.

father, you ask me to marry a woman that you yourself would not marry. she scorns that which i aspire, and that "i" is all my posterity, and i think all there is for those of me who i am yet unaware. no, father, i shall not destroy myself by heeding, diseasing, or even breeding with that pitiful philosophy of life which you are bold enough to base and premise your entire mode of existence.

no, i shall not forget this shit, and talk like i've got some sense, for, you see, my mother bore a mutate—a mutate more capable of surviving past sapiens. i see the both of us for what you and i are, but you should at least be proud, for you were unwittingly the initiating factor. dad, i'm afraid you've—oh, how should i put it? ah, yes—you've created a monster.

soon i shall gobble up all your species, and there will be no more of you. oh, don't worry. It won't be painful. You all had your chance. You see, the curse on Adam and Eve was the same thing. I mean, if you've read your bible, you should know that the devil tempted eve into eating the fruit of knowledge; hence, triggering a fissioning trek to awareness—total awareness—of the Universe. In different words, one would say that adam and eve began evolving; they had made their first motion for being. you see, we are now caught up in a line between that which was not, and that which is. it is so-called evolution that takes us to infinite oneness of all. dad! don't you know that god created man and woman after they ate the apple? How can i say such things? Oh, father! in a way that you could never begin nor want to know.

***

a third of a millennium in our new world has nearly passed, and already we are starved and hungry. when i left you, you had no idea where i was going or what my pioneering journey implied. you advised me to think carefully before doing anything that i might regret, but naturally, in my overly enthusiastic youth, my actions were quick and impulsive, and i considered your advice to be merely the unfortunate skepticism of age. i told you that the values upon which i based my actions were more supreme than yours, due to natural evolution, hence, you could neither advise nor judge me, due to the two total differences in our patterns of thought. i find now that all judgments, despite their nature, are, nay! not false, nor valid, nor anything— they have no being as you might describe it. all our efforts at describing one another by what you know as senses were simply futile.

in our new world we have no language, and no one communicates. this is neither what you call good nor bad. it simply is, as it should be. this i understood before i left, but knowledge and understanding are neither meaningful nor meaningless. they simply are not, which has no positive nor negative connotations, but simply is.

ah! dear mother and father and wife and child! we are just at the end of the first of three millenniums, each being a third of our millennium. i just recalled to myself that you measure. yes, i remember...seconds, minutes, hours, days, years, centuries. what a fantasy! you see, we have no elders nor youngers, no families and no friends. i am total flux until the whole millennium, which is why i am starved and hungry.

i am the shit in the meadows that the cows can eat, but i ca cannot; i am what you kicked at under the table; i am the tear that rolled off my casket; i am all that was up to now, but now the past and the future exist no more, and i am no more until trinity, and All of us breed to make One, and then We shall reunite.

i must prepare you for us. tangential thought: was it an actual period of time and bounded locale that Cro-Magnon replaced Neanderthal? but keep in mind that you don't know where i am nor what i am doing (ha! what i am doing?! a Shakespearean "aside"), but die, and die well, for if you are killed, you are no more, for you have received something that i can't tell you, but you simply can't receive it, and receptacles are merely abysmal vastnesses. thus, eve was condemned before adam, and my purpose is to die to keep you alive, but i have died, and i have lived, and if you are killed, which the serpent would do, I shall be alone, which is the negation, and...! the millennium is a triple multiple of ten. but three over two implies all there is, so, as i remember, you will blow your mind to bits. luckily, you are porifera.

dear mother and father and wife and child.

GAMES

Game i

"Mary, would you like me to fix you a drink?"

"I don't drink."

"That's just fine. Now, would you like me to fix you a drink?"

"Are you capable of it?"

"Only if you want it."

"Very well. I certainly wouldn't want to incapacitate you. I'll have a glass of tap water. Cold, of course. And try to find a clean glass for it."

"That's much better ... here you are, my dear."

"Eh... I nod my head with approval."

"So I noticed. But, my darling, wasn't my extreme adequacy one of the things that attracted you to me when we first met, or have you forgotten already? And we have had such a scintillating relationship. By the way, is your mother attending the séance?"

"That's 'Mother', my dear. Please, try not to forget that so often. It's almost as if you do it deliberately merely to try to provoke me. And one shouldn't do one's loved ones that way. I mean... 'do unto others'..."

"Yes, I agree. Things will change during the séance. I promise. And, as a matter of fact, your moth ... your Mother...and i relate to one another quite well. But, then, it may be due to your catalytic presence."

"You're being mean again, and you know how deeply that upsets me."

"I AM sorry, my dear. It's the water, you know. The guests have arrived. Shall we lead them to the study?"

"Yes, but please act right."

"You know I will, my dear."

Game ii

"You know, Weston. You've changed my whole outlook on things recently. Before you and I got to talking things over, I was really quite confused as to what direction I should do next."

"Well, Bob, as I told you, I firmly believe in human compatibility and total communication among fellow humans. I mean, really, we are all brothers frying in the same frying pan together. Our goal is to find a way out of the frying pan, avoid the fire, and turn the heat off that was under us. Once this is done, mankind's long-desired utopia will have arrived, and we can cast off the burdens of life, and live in total luxury."

"You certainly must have given mankind's ultimate destiny much thought. Oh! How I only wish that I could jump into the future that you describe, right now."

"Have patience, my friend. All God-fearing men will reunite at that celestial apex, where all of Heaven's beings play eternally."

"Do they play craps, and poker, and black jack, and bet the horses? Or do they skip around merrily and freely, like a bunch of queers in a nudist colony? Or do they simply play with one another's minds, so that they will be blasted back into an existence that they will eventually be freed, by self-preservation, to neither accept nor reject, but simply be that? And when this feat of human mercy is undergone, will you and your kind crawl with bare hands and bare asses, and plant yourselves in the dirt, and grow, or will you sprout angelic wings, and flap off into the blue horizon? You know not what you speak nor do. And, brother—as you so convincingly put it—you

154

know not what you think nor are. but how could you? you know not what you are. Now, go kiss that black man, and speak to him as you might speak to yourself. For brotherhood is only your most selfish and intimate thoughts told to you by that man your precious and sacred Jesus would describe as a black, greasy, funky-butt nigger. My friend, you reek of the past, and my soul will not, cannot, nor must not measure time. I wish not to be cynical or hateful, but merely to convey to you that which must eventually be you. Ha! May your life be well fulfilled, and may you walk on water from here to the time you sink."

"Poor sinner. May God have mercy on your soul."

Game iii

sailing along this moonlit night,

thinking of you,

pondering the situation,

i pause, only to reflect

the images that the moon

cast upon my tear-dropped face.

i marvel at the impure, speckled darkness

and at a moon across which, i know,

the silhouettes of countless sky-bound, broom-

boarded witches have flown.

and, to which, many a beautiful young maiden have

been burned at the stake.

How pure and sensitive a death!

To go up in smoke and pollute the
atmosphere for eternity. Why, the secrets of life lie
in our own earthly haze, in the fumes of those who
were crucified and raised to Heaven.

No good does cremation do. Hell! If I can't
use my own incinerator in my own back yard, why
should some priest get paid to burn a corpse, and not
be fired?

I don't understand you people. Maybe because the night is in speckled darkness, and the moon is singing in one-quarter time, that my whole attention and concentration is cleverly lured away from you. Who is the tricky one? Why, me! For i wish to stay alive, so i content myself with the starry, quarter moon lit night, and i purge my mind of other such unearthly thoughts, such as, Who is really "The Man?" or How do I go about obtaining the means to shoot down that helicopter that is pitter-pattering above me, watching me; how do i go about destroying all those who put it up there; how do i go about preventing their further perpetuation and existence.

I'll have no more of their inflictions upon me; I'll have no more revolutions, for there will be no more positives and negatives, no more truth and falsies, no more right and wrong. With one squeeze of my right hand, i reduce them to pulpy, bone-ridden gore. With my left hand, i scoop up the still warm, red, pulsating, germy mold, and gargle with it. It drips from the hair on my chiny-chin-chin, and freezes into droplets of scabby little icicles. I now have no more use for my hands.

my sadness and happiness have vanished, and you are no longer a thing of mind.

Rebuttal i

"It feels so fenced in, Robert. It's almost as if it were meant this way."

"Strange enough, Julie, I feel exactly the same way. Yet still, there are no fences here. These are quite the wide open spaces, and fences are not allowed in wide open space."

"Not allowed? What do you mean? Wide open space would not be wide open space if there Were fences.

"Fences? Where?"

"Why? In wide open space, of course."

"But you said wide open space would not be wide open space if there were fences, therefore, the fences must exist elsewhere besides wide open space."

"But what is there besides wide open space?"

"Closed-in space."

"Closed-in space?! Relative to what?"

"Ah! Now you've introduced a new factor---relativity. So, since you did that, I wish to interject that it seems to me that there is a difference between What space the fence is in, Where is the fence, The space in which it exists, and The space that it occupies. Any of these factors can be arranged in any permutation that you are willing to compute. I wish to add, also, that we are dealing with concepts having three-dimensional confines. Ah—wait now—I detected a grimace. I think I can read your mind. You were getting ready to say, 'Well, what is the actual concept in the mind itself?' And I answer you in saying that concepts, of any kind, and in any proportion, retain their dimensionality, even in the brain, or mind, as you please. The basis for this reasoning is the chemical essence of the mind, itself. The mind is quite material, and quite three-dimensional."

"But what of the intricacies of the mind."

"Merely functioning parts, in a functioning order, functioning in a unique, but functional, manner."

"Then how do we know of another space besides a space which we intuit or conceive in our minds? For remember, all that exists in the mind is three dimensional."

"True. Essentially, that is what I said. But I did not say that all that does exist, exists in the mind."

"Then, where?"

"Where is a word denoting dimension."

"Then we can't talk about it?"

"No. Not until we find the fences."

Rebuttal ii

"Why are you looking so sad?"

"Why am I looking so sad? Because the fountain has died."

"You need not be so unhappy. It was merely turned off temporarily, and I have it from a fairly reputable source that it will be turned on shortly."

"Were they fair when they killed the poor fountain...oh! my poor fountain ... oh! my poor dear fountain. You'll never return to me again!"

"Calm yourself. You shouldn't have dumped the soap in there, anyway."

"But it was dirty and polluted. I only wished to cleanse and purify it."

"You killed the fountain. You killed it with your notions of sterilization; you polluted and diseased it with your ammonia and lyes; you extracted from it what nature had painstakingly injected. A clean fountain? A lifeless fountain, I say! And there you stand, shoulders hunched, sniveling at the misguided potency of your venomous deed."

"How can you be so harsh and cruel? I loved the fountain. Don't you know that?"

"The cruelty you condemn is a fondness that I have cherished for the fountain, despite the harsh and foul blows that you have tended to it. It is your void, not mine. My love persists!"

"Can you revitalize it?"

"Yes. But it will never live again. You must excuse me, for I am off to seek out new life."

"But wait! You said 'new life'. I wasn't aware such a thing exists."

"Then you don't live."

"But I do live, and death is common to all."

"Have you died?"

"No."

"Then death is new; my statement follows."

"If you are right, then my statement of unawareness is correct. The flux of life creates increments of newness, of which I was unaware. Oh! Dear sir! You have helped me so much!"

"But life and death are, themselves, among those increments."

"But..."

"You just destroyed it."

Rebuttal iii

"I wonder why spies catch so much hell during wartime?"

"Spies catch hell all the time."

"Yeah. Why?"

"Spying is the essence of deceiving, and deception is Evil. To deceive is to pledge allegiance to the devil. Mankind had been repudiated to 'give the devil hell,' if you please, but this is folly, for Hell is not for mankind to give."

"Then all men are spies?"

"Exactly! All men are deceivers, not only of other men, but also of themselves. Look around you, and see all the masks and false faces. See all the laughs, smiles, and the personalities and characters, all the habits and idiosyncrasies, all the intellects and speeches. Look at them! And when you're finished looking, try to be angelic, and see where it gets you. I want

your care; not your rotten, superfluous periphery
that may drive you mad."

"Are you calling these things bad?"

"I make no value judgments."

"Save me then."

"Very well." Bang.

III

first i am sad, then miserable, then happy, then
elated. no, not elated. just happy. that's good
enough. if i were elated, i would be wasting needed
energy, energy for illusion, fancy, and defense. but
in defense of what? from whom? what manner of
man or beast is close enough to me to merit my
defense from it? north. east. south. west. Nothing. I
am close to me, but what direction do I focus my
attention to perceive any potential threat? I am at
odds with myself; therefore, I pose a potential
threat? yeow! I have just defined myself as an
enemy and predator to myself. i am concerned with
my well-being and safety, so i must protect myself
from me, and somehow destroy me in order to
remain safe and free from harm. now wait a minute.
how can i be my only enemy? somehow i was
convinced by some outside force, that i am my only
enemy. very conniving, these outside forces! it, or
they? my god, I hope it's not "they" who wish to
cleverly lure me into a state of dangerous, even
suicidal, paranoia. they are the paranoids; they are

the malicious schemers. ha! they're good as dead. all of them. but then what? then there is me. no states of mind. these are superfluous whimsies, standardized by other states of mind. oh boy, what they go through to organize the world they live in. they create vast networks of knowledge, merely to balance and correct that which they have already destroyed. i am the strong one, and i have survived since conception without all their concoctions and mysticisms. I AM THE PRODUCE OF THE UNIVERSE. and when i do see the light of day, and the darkness of night, i shall always be what i am, for that is all there is.

TRINITY

i - Loneliness

<u>Setting:</u> A room—a square, blank white room. I mean white and blank! Everything. No windows. No visible entrances or exits. The corners of the walls, undetectable. No shadows. The room temperature is comfortable.

Dead center, a kneeling, hunched, contorted, decrepit human figure. I observe him at a forty-five degree approach at approximately one foot per second toward his front. The room is thirty feet square. I halt after thirteen seconds. He is totally unaware of my presence. He is pale and naked, and lacking of any body hair. He groans and whimpers to himself. I listen. He starts with a verse from Rime of the Ancient Mariner.

"Day...after day... after day...after day...we struck nor breath ... nor motion ... as idle ... as a painted ship ... upon a painted ocean."

Agonized scream

"Ahhhh. Oh Lord! Why does my kind make its own hell? I can't stand it! It hurts. I want my mommy."

From cries of longing and contorted weeping, he suddenly straightens himself.

"No. I must keep myself together. They want me to do this. they? This? There is only me; no 'this' or 'they' to share the pain. Pain? Where? This room is comfortable. I am comfortable. I am comfortable? What room? What comfort? Who feeds me?"

Still kneeling, he looks about in erratic alertness.

"Where are you? Who are you? What are you? Damn you. Do you hear me? Damn you! Do you have ears? Oh what the fuck. You know what I'm doing, even if you can't really hear me. I mean, what is sound anyway, but waves of hotter air? Fuck you! Is there only one of you? Poor you. You must be horny as hell. Well, you can't fuck me. I'm no faggot! Or are you a woman? Then you really need a fuck. Then you might open the door and let me out, or in, or..."

Sudden change of mood. This time, frantic, pleading. He attempts to stand

"I can't walk. Ahhh! I can't walk. You crippled me, you demigod! Ohh (in agony) only you and me. (breathless and defeated) You feed me; I feed you. What a world. No gods. Nothing to sense or question. No colors, or sounds, or surfaces, or tastes. Just you and me to the better end, eh?" (

He hesitates with anxiety.

"Are you there?"

ii - Love

Setting: center stage-two chairs facing one another. Man and woman seated.

Man: (said bitterly, but with calm) Your conception marked your mother's last happy moment. Your father must be a very cruel man.

Woman: You sniveling, wiry little imp. My father was at least man enough to conceive! You can't even fart right.

Man: (begins looking at her very smugly and self-confidently. He raises his eyebrow.)

My! You have improved. Now laugh this off.
(He raises his hand authoritatively, and briskly
snaps his fingers once. A man enters from left stage
from seated man's rear with an envelope on a metal
platter. He gives the seated man the envelope and
exits in the same way. Seated man, still smugly
smirking, takes the envelope with a flick of the
wrist; he rips open the envelope, snatches out its
contents, smiles, and coolly faces the audience.)
Ladies and gentlemen, I'd like to inform you of a
startling bulletin. A concealed, record-breaking fact
has just been uncovered. (He motions to her,
sweeping his hand). She is the only aborted fetus to
have ever survived. (Meanwhile, woman has
remained completely expressionless and
unemotional).

Woman: (blankly) Are you finished?

 Man: (sardonically) Why, yes!

Woman: Now, tell me, you little weaselly,
disgusting man. Am I supposed to be impressed?
You've exemplified how small your thinking really
is. Aren't you proud of yourself...little man? Or do

you even know what pride is? You prissy little bastard. (Reaches in her purse and pulls out a gun. Gives it to him, executed calmly and without emotion) Here.

Man: (He reaches in his pocket and pulls out a handkerchief. He takes the gun with handkerchief. He snaps his fingers as before. Man comes out with a tray and collects the gun and handkerchief.) Input and output. Equilibrium, the way of nature. Understand that, my dear, and you won't be so predictable. (He smirks, pushes the chair back, and begins to exit left stage. At mid-left, she speaks.)

Woman: I love you. (Said thoughtfully, but deliberately.)

Man: (He stops, somewhat abruptly, stunned, pivots around slowly, and blurts.)
You little bitch! (low, bitter, and slowly. Pause. He grins.) But it is our form of love, isn't it?

iii - Godliness

Setting: An emanance of blinding light.

ha! you mortals! you decrepit, scrawny, pathetic little weak ones. how you cower in your own bloodless, malignant marrow. but, no! i speak of you with feeling, with some depth, with some inner state. My own folly. But then, it would have to be as such anyway.

help me. don't destroy me. i am your last and only link to your special future and your nonexistent past. myths hold; i hold. don't destroy me! i am that zeus; i am that helena; i am that olympus you all crave. i can show you; i can teach you (long pause). i can even evolve you. resolve yourself to seek me out. i am there to kill, you know, and i am there to heal, for you made your own sickness, and what you make, you can destroy.

i want to cry out in pain. i always feel pain. the chambers of my mind echo with torment. Torment? A lack of something, or a negative of something? or is there a difference?

I must gain your trust, so i am groping for your knowledge. Trust me and the simplest things of our universe will be at your command.

ADVENT

the dawn light breaks into all its parts,

and wide-eyed birds

wing their way across Apollo's sun,

and flash their silver-crusted wings

at the reflection of the earth below,

and all god's unjudged relatives

seem to rest in decreasing corporeality.

but the birds at wing,

and the children at seed

differ only within the dawn and dusk

that are common to both,

and so it happens that judgment should occur,

since dusk is not just the absence of dawn—

it is dusk.

in life, there is life;

in death there is death;

death does not over-shadow life,

nor does life precede death.

they are bird and seed,

in dawn and dusk.

in note of a fatherly memorandum:
love only what you can love,
and do not be deceived by guilt and hope,
for they both emerged from the same box,
and they can only return together.

do not brood over what is not,
for what was, is no more,
and never will be.
guilt is the fatal link to the past,
and if eaten and choked down,
can only fuck you up,
fucking and rotting you
with merciless grief, misery, and shame,
producing massive, cancerous boils
throughout the structure of your soul,
and stagnating your very essence—
but the soul of an adventurer is always.

to grieve your own, unfounded guilt is punitive;
to grieve the immortality of a free-spirited man
is truly the only sin there is.

for as it should be,

absence makes the heart grow fonder,

and death can only mean a fondness that

is without end or limit.

now and tomorrow are the times to be fond,

because all the fondness,

lack of fondness,

understanding, and lack of it,

are all states of mind that exist solely in the past,

and are as empty as the past itself.

ESSENCE

i am inspired by simple things. Things like music, insects, wind, water, trees, concrete, stone, children, and mankind. i dream of flying. I have never dreamed of falling.

I don't chase, nor do I injure, harm, maim, assault, threaten, cripple, or inflict myself upon. I don't kill. I don't heal. I don't thrash, give, nor rob. I don't reward, praise, creditate, preditate, punish, nor execute. I don't judge. I will never play a harp and I will never burn.

I do fly—and that is all I do.

***

and i see the messenger cruise in leaps and bounds in the dale that surrounds me, and the messenger flies toward me to bring me the news that we are free, that we no longer bear the chains and shackles of our people, and being not of them, we can free them, and make them well, for the cure is a natural one, spawned by Love, and nurtured by the carcasses of the parting diseased sickness. and the messenger whirls round me, cascading the joy of my people into every morsel of my body. and i now with all my sinew to show my pleasure, for it is not a momentary pleasure—a sickness—but a thing that my people lost only a yesterday that refused to allow tomorrow. today is here, and we can be assured of tomorrow, for tomorrow is the least of all dreams. it is the essence of my people, lest my people be dreams, and my universe and myself be deceivers—and this is not.

Cy Tyler opened the door. His seizure of indecision was momentary. He carried himself through the door effortlessly. The air was nauseatingly heavy and sticky, coated with the smell of lingering old food for tasteless old people.

He walked across a noisy unwaxed, slat floor, decorated by the yellow dinginess of the flicking gas lamp that shadowed the restaurant.

The wail of the infant continued.

baby, baby, don't you cry. papa is comin! papa's gonna love you. papa all you got. please. baby, baby, don't you cry. today got to be the happiest day o' yo life. you were born today. lil' baby was born today; lil' baby'll die tomorrow. so cry tomorrow, lil' baby, not today.

A plane of light split his path, and disappeared. A black figure stood, leaning on the door, confronting Cy. all i want is freedom, just life. why people got to die to be free?

Cy, your wife died in child-birth. She called for you. You weren't there. She's dead—and so are you.